"A PLEASING LITTLE PROBLEM, OBSCURE AND CHARMING," POIROT MURMURED. "MADAM, I WILL INVESTIGATE IT FOR YOU...."

The legendary Hercule Poirot's powers are taxed to the limit as he grapples with a kidnapper so arrogant, he announces his intentions beforehand . . . a murderer who leaves abundant clues . . . and an eccentric who changes the habits of a lifetime—the day before "accidentally" plunging to his death.

Poirot is joined by the ever-astonishing Miss Jane Marple—and by Mr. Harley Quin, that most sartorial of detectives. Together, they provide that blend of suspense and ingenuity that has long distinguished Agatha Christie as a writer of mysteries without equal.

Other Agatha Christie Titles
Currently Available in Dell Editions

Three Blind Mice
and Other Stories

(formerly published as *The Mousetrap*)

AGATHA CHRISTIE

A DELL BOOK

Published by
DELL PUBLISHING CO., INC.
1 Dag Hammarskjold Plaza
New York, New York 10017

ISBN: 0-440-15867-2

Reprinted by arrangement with
Dodd, Mead & Company, Inc.
Printed in the United States of America
Previous Dell Edition #5860
First printing—May 1977
Second printing—July 1977
Third printing—November 1977
Fourth printing—May 1978
Fifth printing—November 1978
New Dell Edition
First printing—July 1980

Contents

Three Blind Mice

Three Blind Mice

See how they run

See how they run

They all ran after the farmer's wife

She cut off their tails with a carving knife

Did you ever see such a sight in your life

As THREE BLIND MICE

Three Blind Mice

IT WAS VERY COLD. The sky was dark and heavy with unshed snow.

A man in a dark overcoat, with his muffler pulled up round his face, and his hat pulled down over his eyes, came along Culver Street and went up the steps of number 74. He put his finger on the bell and heard it shrilling in the basement below.

Mrs. Casey, her hands busy in the sink, said bitterly, "Drat that bell. Never any peace, there isn't."

Wheezing a little, she toiled up the basement stairs and opened the door.

The man standing silhouetted against the lowering sky outside asked in a whisper, "Mrs. Lyon?"

"Second floor," said Mrs. Casey. "You can go on up. Does she expect you?" The man slowly shook his head. "Oh, well, go on up and knock."

She watched him as he went up the shabbily carpeted stairs. Afterward she said he "gave her a funny feeling." But actually all she thought was that he must have a pretty bad cold only to be able to whisper like that—and no wonder with the weather what it was.

When the man got round the bend of the staircase he began to whistle softly. The tune he whistled was "Three Blind Mice."

Molly Davis stepped back into the road and looked up at the newly painted board by the gate.

Monkswell Manor
Guest House

She nodded approval. It looked, it really did look, quite professional. Or, perhaps, one might say *almost* professional. The *T* of *Guest House* staggered uphill a little, and the end of *Manor* was slightly crowded, but on the whole Giles had made a wonderful job of it. Giles was really very clever. There were so many things that he could do. She was always making fresh discoveries about this husband of hers. He said so little about himself that it was only by degrees that she was finding out what a lot of varied talents he had. An ex-naval man was always a "handy man," so people said.

Well, Giles would have need of all his talents in their new venture. Nobody could be more raw to the business of running a guest house than she and Giles. But it would be great fun. And it did solve the housing problem.

It had been Molly's idea. When Aunt Katherine died, and the lawyers wrote to her and informed her that her aunt had left her Monkswell Manor, the natural reaction of the young couple had been to sell it. Giles had asked, "What is it like?" And Molly had replied, "Oh, a big, rambling old house, full of stuffy, old-fashioned Victorian furniture. Rather a nice garden, but terribly overgrown since the war, because there's been only one old gardener left."

So they had decided to put the house on the market, and keep just enough furniture to furnish a small cottage or flat for themselves.

But two difficulties arose at once. First, there *weren't* any small cottages or flats to be found, and secondly, all the furniture was enormous.

"Well," said Molly, "we'll just have to sell it *all*. I suppose it *will* sell?"

The solicitor assured them that nowadays *anything* would sell.

"Very probably," he said, "someone will buy it for a

hotel or guest house in which case they might like to buy it with the furniture complete. Fortunately the house is in very good repair. The late Miss Emory had extensive repairs and modernizations done just before the war, and there has been very little deterioration. Oh, yes, it's in good shape."

And it was then that Molly had had her idea.

"Giles," she said, "why shouldn't *we* run it as a guest house ourselves?"

At first her husband had scoffed at the idea, but Molly had persisted.

"We needn't take very many people—not at first. It's an easy house to run—it's got hot and cold water in the bedrooms and central heating and a gas cooker. And we can have hens and ducks and our own eggs, and vegetables."

"Who'd do all the work—isn't it very hard to get servants?"

"Oh, *we'd* have to do the work. But wherever we lived we'd have to do that. A few extra people wouldn't really mean much more to do. We'd probably get a woman to come in after a bit when we got properly started. If we had only five people, each paying seven guineas a week—" Molly departed into the realms of somewhat optimistic mental arithmetic.

"And think, Giles," she ended, "it would be our *own* house. With our *own* things. As it is, it seems to me it will be years before we can ever find anywhere to live."

That, Giles admitted, was true. They had had so little time together since their hasty marriage, that they were both longing to settle down in a home.

So the great experiment was set under way. Advertisements were put in the local paper and in the *Times,* and various answers came.

And now, today, the first of the guests was to arrive.

Giles had gone off early in the car to try and obtain some army wire netting that had been advertised as for sale on the other side of the county. Molly announced the necessity of walking to the village to make some last purchases.

The only thing that was wrong was the weather. For the last two days it had been bitterly cold, and now the snow was beginning to fall. Molly hurried up the drive, thick, feathery flakes falling on her waterproofed shoulders and bright curly hair. The weather forecasts had been lugubrious in the extreme. Heavy snowfall was to be expected.

She hoped anxiously that all the pipes wouldn't freeze. It would be too bad if everything went wrong just as they started. She glanced at her watch. Past teatime. Would Giles have got back yet? Would he be wondering where *she* was?

"I had to go to the village again for something I had forgotten," she would say. And he would laugh and say, "More tins?"

Tins were a joke between them. They were always on the lookout for tins of food. The larder was really quite nicely stocked now in case of emergencies.

And, Molly thought with a grimace as she looked up at the sky, it looked as though emergencies were going to present themselves very soon.

The house was empty. Giles was not back yet. Molly went first into the kitchen, then upstairs, going round the newly prepared bedrooms. Mrs. Boyle in the south room with the mahogany and the four-poster. Major Metcalf in the blue room with the oak. Mr. Wren in the east room with the bay window. All the rooms looked very nice— and what a blessing that Aunt Katherine had had such a splendid stock of linen. Molly patted a counterpane into place and went downstairs again. It was nearly dark.

The house felt suddenly very quiet and empty. It was a lonely house, two miles from a village, two miles, as Molly put it, from *anywhere*.

She had often been alone in the house before—but she had never before been so conscious of being alone in it.

The snow beat in a soft flurry against the window-panes. It made a whispery, uneasy sound. Supposing Giles couldn't get back—supposing the snow was so thick that the car couldn't get through? Supposing she had to stay alone here—stay alone for days, perhaps.

She looked round the kitchen—a big, comfortable kitchen that seemed to call for a big, comfortable cook presiding at the kitchen table, her jaws moving rhythmically as she ate rock cakes and drank black tea—she should be flanked by a tall, elderly parlormaid on one side and a round, rosy housemaid on the other, with a kitchenmaid at the other end of the table observing her betters with frightened eyes. And instead there was just herself, Molly Davis, playing a role that did not yet seem a very natural role to play. Her whole life, at the moment, seemed unreal—Giles seemed unreal. She was playing a part—just playing a part.

A shadow passed the window, and she jumped—a strange man was coming through the snow. She heard the rattle of the side door. The stranger stood there in the open doorway, shaking off snow, a strange man, walking into the empty house.

And then, suddenly, illusion fled.

"Oh Giles," she cried, "I'm so glad you've come!"

"Hullo, sweetheart! What filthy weather! Lord, I'm *frozen*."

He stamped his feet and blew through his hands.

Automatically Molly picked up the coat that he had thrown in a Giles-like manner onto the oak chest. She put it on a hanger, taking out of the stuffed pockets a muffler, a newspaper, a ball of string, and the morning's correspondence which he had shoved in pell-mell. Moving into the kitchen, she laid down the articles on the dresser and put the kettle on the gas.

"Did you get the netting?" she asked. "What ages you've been."

"It wasn't the right kind. Wouldn't have been any good for us. I went on to another dump, but that wasn't any good, either. What have you been doing with yourself? Nobody turned up yet, I suppose?"

"Mrs. Boyle isn't coming till tomorrow, anyway."

"Major Metcalf and Mr. Wren ought to be here today."

"Major Metcalf sent a card to say he wouldn't be here till tomorrow."

"Then that leaves us and Mr. Wren for dinner. What do you think he's like? Correct sort of retired civil servant is my idea."

"No, I think he's an artist."

"In that case," said Giles, "we'd better get a week's rent in advance."

"Oh, no, Giles, they bring luggage. If they don't pay we hang on to their luggage."

"And suppose their luggage is stones wrapped up in newspaper? The truth is, Molly, we don't in the least know what we're up against in this business. I hope they don't spot what beginners we are."

"Mrs. Boyle is sure to," said Molly. "She's that kind of woman."

"How do you know? You haven't seen her?"

Molly turned away. She spread a newspaper on the table, fetched some cheese, and set to work to grate it.

"What's this?" inquired her husband.

"It's going to be Welsh rarebit," Molly informed him.

"Bread crumbs and mashed potatoes and just a *teeny weeny* bit of cheese to justify its name."

"Aren't you a clever cook?" said her admiring husband.

"I wonder. I can do one thing at a time. It's *assembling* them that needs so much practice. Breakfast is the worst."

"Why?"

"Because it all happens at once—eggs and bacon and hot milk and coffee and toast. The milk boils over, or the toast burns, or the bacon frizzles, or the eggs go hard. You have to be as active as a scalded cat watching everything at once."

"I shall have to creep down unobserved tomorrow morning and watch this scalded-cat impersonation."

"The kettle's boiling," said Molly. "Shall we take the tray into the library and hear the wireless? It's almost time for the news."

"As we seem to be going to spend almost the whole of our time in the kitchen, we ought to have a wireless there, too."

"Yes. How nice kitchens are. I love this kitchen. I think it's far and away the nicest room in the house. I like the dresser and the plates, and I simply love the lavish feeling that an absolutely *enormous* kitchen range gives you—though, of course, I'm thankful I haven't got to cook on it."

"I suppose a whole year's fuel ration would go in one day."

"Almost certainly, I should say. But think of the great joints that were roasted in it—sirloins of beef and saddles of mutton. Colossal copper preserving-pans full of home-made strawberry jam with pounds and pounds of sugar going into it. What a lovely, comfortable age the Victorian age was. Look at the furniture upstairs, large and solid and rather ornate—but, oh!—the heavenly comfort of it, with lots of room for the clothes one used to have, and every drawer sliding in and out so easily. Do you remember that smart modern flat we were lent? Everything built in and sliding—only nothing slid—it always stuck. And the doors pushed shut—only they never stayed shut, or if they did shut they wouldn't open."

"Yes, that's the worst of gadgets. If they don't go right, you're sunk."

"Well, come on, let's hear the news."

The news consisted mainly of grim warnings about the weather, the usual deadlock in foreign affairs, spirited bickerings in Parliament, and a murder in Culver Street, Paddington.

"Ugh," said Molly, switching it off. "Nothing but misery. I'm *not* going to hear appeals for fuel economy all over again. What do they expect you to do, sit and freeze? I don't think we ought to have tried to start a guest house in the winter. We ought to have waited until the spring." She added in a different tone of voice, "I wonder what the woman was like who was murdered."

"Mrs. Lyon?"

"Was that her name? I wonder who wanted to murder her and why."

"Perhaps she had a fortune under the floor boards."

"When it says the police are anxious to interview a man 'seen in the vicinity' does that mean he's the murderer?"

"I think it's usually that. Just a polite way of putting it."

The shrill note of a bell made them both jump.

"That's the front door," said Giles. "Enter—a murderer," he added facetiously.

"It would be, of course, in a play. Hurry up. It must be Mr. Wren. Now we shall see who's right about him, you or me."

Mr. Wren and a flurry of snow came in together with

a rush. All that Molly, standing in the library door, could see of the newcomer was his silhouette against the white world outside.

How alike, thought Molly, were all men in their livery of civilization. Dark overcoat, gray hat, muffler round the neck.

In another moment Giles had shut the front door against the elements, Mr. Wren was unwinding his muffler and casting down his suitcase and flinging off his hat —all, it seemed, at the same time, and also talking. He had a high-pitched, almost querulous voice and stood revealed in the light of the hall as a young man with a shock of light, sunburned hair and pale, restless eyes.

"Too, too frightful," he was saying. "The English winter at its worst—a reversion to Dickens—Scrooge and Tiny Tim and all that. One had to be so terribly hearty to stand up to it all. Don't you think so? And I've had a terrible cross-country journey from Wales. Are you Mrs. Davis? But how delightful!" Molly's hand was seized in a quick, bony clasp. "Not at all as I'd imagined you. I'd pictured you, you know, as an Indian army general's widow. Terrifically grim and *mem-sahibish*—and Benares *whatnot*—a real Victorian *whatnot*. Heavenly, simply heavenly— Have you got any wax flowers? Or birds of paradise? Oh, but I'm simply going to *love* this place. I was afraid, you know, it would be very Olde Worlde— very, very Manor House—failing the Benares brass, I mean. Instead, it's marvelous—real Victorian bedrock respectability. Tell me, have you got one of those beautiful sideboards—mahogany—purple-plummy mahogany with great carved fruits?"

"As a matter of fact," said Molly, rather breathless under this torrent of words, "we have."

"No! Can I see it? At once. In here?"

His quickness was almost disconcerting. He had turned

the handle of the dining-room door, and clicked on the light. Molly followed him in, conscious of Giles's disapproving profile on her left.

Mr. Wren passed his long bony fingers over the rich carving of the massive sideboard with little cries of appreciation. Then he turned a reproachful glance upon his hostess.

"No big mahogany dining-table? All these little tables dotted about instead?"

"We thought people would prefer it that way," said Molly.

"Darling, of course you're *quite* right. I was being carried away by my feeling for period. Of course, if you had the table, you'd have to have the right family round it. Stern, handsome father with a beard—prolific, faded mother, eleven children, a grim governess, and somebody called 'poor Harriet'—the poor relation who acts as general helper and is very, very grateful for being given a good home. Look at that grate—think of the flames leaping up the chimney and blistering poor Harriet's back."

"I'll take your suitcase upstairs," said Giles. "East room?"

"Yes," said Molly.

Mr. Wren skipped out into the hall again as Giles went upstairs.

"Has it got a four-poster with little chintz roses?" he asked.

"No, it hasn't," said Giles and disappeared round the bend of the staircase.

"I don't believe your husband is going to like me," said Mr. Wren. "What's he been in? The navy?"

"Yes."

"I thought so. They're much less tolerant than the army and the air force. How long have you been married? Are you very much in love with him?"

"Perhaps you'd like to come up and see your room."

"Yes, of course that was impertinent. But I did really want to know. I mean, it's interesting, don't you think, to know all about people? What they feel and think, I mean, not just who they are and what they do."

"I suppose," said Molly in a demure voice, "you are Mr. Wren?"

The young man stopped short, clutched his hair in both hands and tugged at it.

"But how frightful—I never put first things first. Yes, I'm Christopher Wren—now, don't laugh. My parents were a romantic couple. They hoped I'd be an architect. So they thought it a splendid idea to christen me Christopher—halfway home, as it were."

"And are you an architect?" asked Molly, unable to help smiling.

"Yes, I am," said Mr. Wren triumphantly. "At least I'm nearly one. I'm not fully qualified yet. But it's really a remarkable example of wishful thinking coming off for once. Mind you, actually the name will be a handicap. I shall never be *the* Christopher Wren. However, Chris Wren's Pre-Fab Nests may achieve fame."

Giles came down the stairs again, and Molly said, "I'll show you your room now, Mr. Wren."

When she came down a few minutes later, Giles said, "Well, did he like the pretty oak furniture?"

"He was very anxious to have a four-poster, so I gave him the rose room instead."

Giles grunted and murmured something that ended, ". . . young twerp."

"Now, look here, Giles," Molly assumed a severe demeanor. "This isn't a house party of guests we're entertaining. This is business. Whether you like Christopher Wren or not—"

"I don't," Giles interjected.

"—has nothing whatever to do with it. He's paying seven guineas a week, and that's all that matters."

"If he pays it, yes."

"He's agreed to pay it. We've got his letter."

"Did you transfer that suitcase of his to the rose room?"

"He carried it, of course."

"Very gallant. But it wouldn't have strained you. There's certainly no question of stones wrapped up in newspaper. It's so light that there seems to me there's probably nothing in it."

"*Ssh,* here he comes," said Molly warningly.

Christopher Wren was conducted to the library which looked, Molly thought, very nice, indeed, with its big chairs and its log fire. Dinner, she told him, would be in half an hour's time. In reply to a question, she explained that there were no other guests at the moment. In that case, Christopher said, how would it be if he came into the kitchen and helped?

"I can cook you an omelette if you like," he said engagingly.

The subsequent proceedings took place in the kitchen, and Christopher helped with the washing up.

Somehow, Molly felt, it was not quite the right start for a conventional guest house—and Giles had not liked it at all. Oh, well, thought Molly, as she fell asleep, to-morrow when the others came it would be different.

The morning came with dark skies and snow. Giles looked grave, and Molly's heart fell. The weather was going to make everything very difficult.

Mrs. Boyle arrived in the local taxi with chains on the wheels, and the driver brought pessimistic reports of the state of the road.

"Drifts afore nightfall," he prophesied.

Mrs. Boyle herself did not lighten the prevailing

gloom. She was a large, forbidding-looking woman with a resonant voice and a masterful manner. Her natural aggressiveness had been heightened by a war career of persistent and militant usefulness.

"If I had not believed this was a *running* concern, I should never have come," she said. "I naturally thought it was a well-established guest house, properly run on scientific lines."

"There is no obligation for you to remain if you are not satisfied, Mrs. Boyle," said Giles.

"No, indeed, and I shall not think of doing so."

"Perhaps, Mrs. Boyle," said Giles, "you would like to ring up for a taxi. The roads are not yet blocked. If there has been any misapprehension it would, perhaps, be better if you went elsewhere." He added, "We have had so many applications for rooms that we shall be able to fill your place quite easily—indeed, in future we are charging a higher rate for our rooms."

Mrs. Boyle threw him a sharp glance. "I am certainly not going to leave before I have tried what the place is like. Perhaps you would let me have a rather large bath towel, Mrs. Davis. I am not accustomed to drying myself on a pocket handkerchief."

Giles grinned at Molly behind Mrs. Boyle's retreating back.

"Darling, you were wonderful," said Molly. "The way you stood up to her."

"Bullies soon climb down when they get their own medicine," said Giles.

"Oh, dear," said Molly. "I wonder how she'll get on with Christopher Wren."

"She won't," said Giles.

And, indeed, that very afternoon, Mrs. Boyle remarked to Molly, "That's a very peculiar young man," with distinct disfavor in her voice.

The baker arrived looking like an Arctic explorer and delivered the bread with the warning that his next call, due in two days' time, might not materialize.

"Holdups everywhere," he announced. "Got plenty of stores in, I hope?"

"Oh, yes," said Molly. "We've got lots of tins. I'd better take extra flour, though."

She thought vaguely that there was something the Irish made called soda bread. If the worst came to the worst she could probably make that.

The baker had also brought the papers, and she spread them out on the hall table. Foreign affairs had receded in importance. The weather and the murder of Mrs. Lyon occupied the front page.

She was staring at the blurred reproduction of the dead woman's features when Christopher Wren's voice behind her said, "Rather a *sordid* murder, don't you think? Such a *drab*-looking woman and such a *drab* street. One can't feel, can one, that there is any story behind it?"

"I've no doubt," said Mrs. Boyle with a snort, "that the creature got no more than she deserved."

"Oh." Mr. Wren turned to her with engaging eagerness. "So you think it's definitely a *sex* crime, do you?"

"I suggested nothing of the kind, Mr. Wren."

"But she *was* strangled, wasn't she? I wonder—" he held out his long white hands—"what it would feel like to strangle anyone."

"Really, Mr. Wren!"

Christopher moved nearer to her, lowering his voice. "Have you considered, Mrs. Boyle, just what it would feel like to be strangled?"

Mrs. Boyle said again, even more indignantly, "Really, Mr. Wren!"

Molly read hurriedly out, " 'The man the police are

anxious to interview was wearing a dark overcoat and a light Homburg hat, was of medium height, and wore a woolen scarf.' "

"In fact," said Christopher Wren, "he looked just like everybody else." He laughed.

"Yes," said Molly. "Just like everybody else."

In his room at Scotland Yard, Inspector Parminter said to Detective Sergeant Kane, "I'll see those two workmen now."

"Yes, sir."

"What are they like?"

"Decent class workingmen. Rather slow reactions. Dependable."

"Right." Inspector Parminter nodded.

Presently two embarrassed-looking men in their best clothes were shown into his room. Parminter summed them up with a quick eye. He was an adept at setting people at their ease.

"So you think you've some information that might be useful to us on the Lyon case," he said. "Good of you to come along. Sit down. Smoke?"

He waited while they accepted cigarettes and lit up.

"Pretty awful weather outside."

"It is that, sir."

"Well, now, then—let's have it."

The two men looked at each other, embarrassed now that it came to the difficulties of narration.

"Go ahead, Joe," said the bigger of the two.

Joe went ahead. "It was like this, see. We 'adn't got a match."

"Where was this?"

"Jarman Street—we was working on the road there—gas mains."

Inspector Parminter nodded. Later he would get down

to exact details of time and place. Jarman Street, he knew was in the close vicinity of Culver Street where the tragedy had taken place.

"You hadn't got a match," he repeated encouragingly.

"No. Finished my box, I 'ad, and Bill's lighter wouldn't work, and so I spoke to a bloke as was passing. 'Can you give us a match, mister?' I says. Didn't think nothing particular, I didn't, not then. He was just passing—like lots of others—I just 'appened to arsk 'im."

Again Parminter nodded.

"Well, he give us a match, 'e did. Didn't say nothing. 'Cruel cold,' Bill said to 'im, and he just answered, whispering-like, 'Yes, it is.' Got a cold on his chest, I thought. He was all wrapped up, anyway. 'Thanks, mister,' I says and gives him back his matches, and he moves off quick, so quick that when I sees 'e'd dropped something, it's almost too late to call 'im back. It was a little notebook as he must 'ave pulled out of 'is pocket when he got the matches out. 'Hi, mister,' I calls after 'im, 'you've dropped something.' But he didn't seem to hear—he just quickens up and bolts round the corner, didn't 'e, Bill?"

"That's right," agreed Bill. "Like a scurrying rabbit."

"Into the Harrow Road, that was, and it didn't seem as we'd catch up with him there, not the rate 'e was going, and, anyway, by then it was a bit late—it was only a little book, not a wallet or anything like that—maybe it wasn't important. 'Funny bloke,' I says. 'His hat pulled down over his eyes, and all buttoned up—like a crook on the pictures,' I says to Bill, didn't I, Bill?"

"That's what you said," agreed Bill.

"Funny I should have said that, not that I thought anything at the time. Just in a hurry to get home, that's what I thought, and I didn't blame 'im. Not 'arf cold, it was!"

"Not 'arf," agreed Bill.

"So I says to Bill, 'Let's 'ave a look at this little book and see if it's important.' Well, sir, I took a look. 'Only a couple of addresses,' I says to Bill. Seventy-Four Culver Street and some blinking manor 'ouse."

"Ritzy," said Bill with a snort of disapproval.

Joe continued his tale with a certain gusto now that he had got wound up.

" 'Seventy-Four Culver Street,' I says to Bill. 'That's just round the corner from 'ere. When we knock off, we'll take it round'—and then I sees something written across the top of the page. 'What's this?' I says to Bill. And he takes it and reads it out. ' "Three blind mice"— must be off 'is knocker,' he says—and just at that very moment—yes, it was that very moment, sir, we 'ears some woman yelling, 'Murder!' a couple of streets away!"

Joe paused at this artistic climax.

"Didn't half yell, did she?" he resumed. " 'Here,' I says to Bill, 'you nip along.' And by and by he comes back and says there's a big crowd and the police are there and some woman's had her throat cut or been strangled and that was the landlady who found her, yelling for the police. 'Where was it?' I says to him. 'In Culver Street,' he says. 'What number?' I asks, and he says he didn't rightly notice."

Bill coughed and shuffled his feet with the sheepish air of one who has not done himself justice.

"So I says, 'We'll nip around and make sure,' and when we finds it's number seventy-four we talk it over, and 'Maybe,' Bill says, 'the address in the notebook's got nothing to do with it,' and I says as maybe it *has*, and, anyway, after we've talked it over and heard the police want to interview a man who left the 'ouse about that time, well, we come along 'ere and ask if we can see the gentleman who's handling the case, and I'm sure I 'ope as we aren't wasting your time."

"You acted very properly," said Parminter approvingly. "You've brought the notebook with you? Thank you.
Now—"

His questions became brisk and professional. He got
places, times, dates—the only thing he did not get was
a description of the man who had dropped the notebook.
Instead he got the same description as he had already
got from a hysterical landlady, the description of a hat
pulled down over the eyes, a buttoned-up coat, a muffler
swathed round the lower part of a face, a voice that was
only a whisper, gloved hands.

When the men had gone he remained staring down at
the little book lying open on his table. Presently it would
go to the appropriate department to see what evidence,
if any, of fingerprints it might reveal. But now his attention was held by the two addresses and by the line of
small handwriting along the top of the page.

He turned his head as Sergeant Kane came into the
room.

"Come here, Kane. Look at this."

Kane stood behind him and let out a low whistle as
he read out, " 'Three Blind Mice!' Well, I'm dashed!"

"Yes." Parminter opened a drawer and took out a half
sheet of notepaper which he laid beside the notebook on
his desk. It had been found pinned carefully to the
murdered woman.

On it was written, *This is the first.* Below was a childish drawing of three mice and a bar of music.

Kane whistled the tune softly. *Three Blind Mice, See
how they run—*

"That's it, all right. That's the signature tune."

"Crazy, isn't it, sir?"

"Yes." Parminter frowned. "The identification of the
woman is quite certain?"

"Yes, sir. Here's the report from the fingerprints department. Mrs. Lyon, as she called herself, was really Maureen Gregg. She was released from Holloway two months ago on completion of her sentence."

Parminter said thoughtfully, "She went to Seventy-Four Culver Street calling herself Maureen Lyon. She occasionally drank a bit and she had been known to bring a man home with her once or twice. She displayed no fear of anything or anyone. There's no reason to believe she thought herself in any danger. This man rings the bell, asks for her, and is told by the landlady to go up to the second floor. She can't describe him, says only that he was of medium height and seemed to have a bad cold and lost his voice. She went back again to the basement and heard nothing of a suspicious nature. She did not hear the man go out. Ten minutes or so later she took tea to her lodger and discovered her strangled.

"This wasn't a casual murder, Kane. It was carefully planned." He paused and then added abruptly, "I wonder how many houses there are in England called Monkswell Manor?"

"There might be only one, sir."

"That would probably be too much luck. But get on with it. There's no time to lose."

The sergeant's eye rested appreciatively on two entries in the notebook—*74 Culver Street; Monkswell Manor.*

He said, "So you think—"

Parminter said swiftly, "Yes. Don't you?"

"Could be. Monkswell Manor—now where— Do you know, sir, I could swear I've seen that name quite lately."

"Where?"

"That's what I'm trying to remember. Wait a minute— Newspaper— *Times.* Back page. Wait a minute— Hotels and boardinghouses— Half a sec, sir—it's an old one. I was doing the crossword."

He hurried out of the room and returned in triumph. "Here you are, sir, look."

The inspector followed the pointing finger.

"Monkswell Manor, Harpleden, Berks." He drew the telephone toward him. "Get me the Berkshire County police."

With the arrival of Major Metcalf, Monkswell Manor settled into its routine as a going concern. Major Metcalf was neither formidable like Mrs. Boyle, nor erratic like Christopher Wren. He was a stolid, middle-aged man of spruce military appearance, who had done most of his service in India. He appeared satisfied with his room and its furniture, and while he and Mrs. Boyle did not actually find mutual friends, he had known cousins of friends of hers—"the Yorkshire branch," out in Poonah. His luggage, however, two heavy pigskin cases, satisfied even Giles's suspicious nature.

Truth to tell, Molly and Giles did not have much time for speculating about their guests. Between them, dinner was cooked, served, eaten, and washed up satisfactorily. Major Metcalf praised the coffee, and Giles and Molly retired to bed, tired but triumphant—to be roused about two in the morning by the persistent ringing of a bell.

"Damn," said Giles. "It's the front door. What on earth—"

"Hurry up," said Molly. "Go and see."

Casting a reproachful glance at her, Giles wrapped his dressing-gown round him and descended the stairs. Molly heard the bolts being drawn back and a murmur of voices in the hall. Presently, driven by curiosity, she crept out of bed and went to peep from the top of the stairs. In the hall below, Giles was assisting a bearded stranger out of a snow-covered overcoat. Fragments of conversation floated up to her.

"Brrr." It was an explosive foreign sound. "My fingers are so cold I cannot feel them. And my feet—" A stamping sound was heard.

"Come in here." Giles threw open the library door. "It's warm. You'd better wait here while I get a room ready."

"I am indeed fortunate," said the stranger politely.

Molly peered inquisitively through the banisters. She saw an elderly man with a small black beard and Mephistophelean eyebrows. A man who moved with a young and jaunty step in spite of the gray at his temples.

Giles shut the library door on him and came quickly up the stairs. Molly rose from her crouching position.

"Who is it?" she demanded.

Giles grinned. "Another guest for the guest house. Car overturned in a snowdrift. He got himself out and was making his way as best he could—it's a howling blizzard still, listen to it—along the road when he saw our board. He said it was like an answer to prayer."

"You think he's—all right?"

"Darling, this isn't the sort of night for a housebreaker to be doing his rounds."

"He's a foreigner, isn't he?"

"Yes. His name's Paravicini. I saw his wallet—I rather think he showed it on purpose—simply crammed with notes. Which room shall we give him?"

"The green room. It's all tidy and ready. We'll just have to make up the bed."

"I suppose I'll have to lend him pajamas. All his things are in the car. He said he had to climb out through the window."

Molly fetched sheets, pillowcases, and towels.

As they hurriedly made the bed up, Giles said, "It's coming down thick. We're going to be snowed up, Molly, completely cut off. Rather exciting in a way, isn't it?"

"I don't know," said Molly doubtfully. "Do you think I can make soda bread, Giles?"

"Of course you can. You can make anything," said her loyal husband.

"I've never tried to make bread. It's the sort of thing one takes for granted. It may be new or it may be stale but it's just something the baker brings. But if we're snowed up there won't be a baker."

"Nor a butcher, nor a postman. No newspapers. And probably no telephone."

"Just the wireless telling us what to do?"

"At any rate we make our own electric light."

"You must run the engine again tomorrow. And we must keep the central heating well stoked."

"I suppose our next lot of coke won't come in now. We're very low."

"Oh, bother. Giles, I feel we are in for a simply frightful time. Hurry up and get Para—whatever his name is. I'll go back to bed."

Morning brought confirmation of Giles's forebodings. Snow was piled five feet high, drifting up against the doors and windows. Outside it was still snowing. The world was white, silent, and—in some subtle way—menacing.

Mrs. Boyle sat at breakfast. There was no one else in the dining-room. At the adjoining table, Major Metcalf's place had been cleared away. Mr. Wren's table was still laid for breakfast. One early riser, presumably, and one late one. Mrs. Boyle herself knew definitely that there was only one proper time for breakfast, nine o'clock.

Mrs. Boyle had finished her excellent omelette and was champing toast between her strong white teeth. She was in a grudging and undecided mood. Monkswell Manor was not at all what she had imagined it would be. She had hoped for bridge, for faded spinsters whom she could impress with her social position and connections, and to whom she could hint at the importance and secrecy of her war service.

The end of the war had left Mrs. Boyle marooned, as it were, on a desert shore. She had always been a busy woman, talking fluently of efficiency and organization. Her vigor and drive had prevented people asking whether she was, indeed, a good or efficient organizer. War activities had suited her down to the ground. She had bossed people and bullied people and worried heads of departments and, to give her her due, had at no time spared herself. Subservient women had run to and fro, terrified of her slightest frown. And now all that exciting hustling life was over. She was back in private life, and her former private life had vanished. Her house, which had been requisitioned by the army, needed thorough repairing and redecorating before she could return to it, and the difficulties of domestic help made a return to it impracticable in any case. Her friends were largely scattered and dispersed. Presently, no doubt, she would find her niche, but at the moment it was a case of marking time. A hotel or a boardinghouse seemed the answer. And she had chosen to come to Monkswell Manor.

She looked round her disparagingly.

Most dishonest, she said to herself, *not to have told me they were only just starting.*

She pushed her plate farther away from her. The fact that her breakfast had been excellently cooked and served, with good coffee and homemade marmalade, in a curious way annoyed her still more. It had deprived her of a legitimate cause of complaint. Her bed, too, had been comfortable, with embroidered sheets and a soft pillow. Mrs. Boyle liked comfort, but she also liked to find fault. The latter was, perhaps, the stronger passion of the two.

Rising majestically, Mrs. Boyle left the dining-room, passing in the doorway that very extraordinary young man with the red hair. He was wearing this morning a checked tie of virulent green—a woolen tie.

Preposterous, said Mrs. Boyle to herself. *Quite preposterous.*

The way he looked at her, too, sideways out of those pale eyes of his—she didn't like it. There was something upsetting—unusual—about that faintly mocking glance.

Unbalanced mentally, I shouldn't wonder, said Mrs. Boyle to herself.

She acknowledged his flamboyant bow with a slight inclination of her head and marched into the big drawing-room. Comfortable chairs here, particularly the large rose-colored one. She had better make it clear that that was to be *her* chair. She deposited her knitting on it as a precaution and walked over and laid a hand on the radiators. As she had suspected, they were only warm, not hot. Mrs. Boyle's eye gleamed militantly. She could have something to say about *that.*

She glanced out of the window. Dreadful weather— quite dreadful. Well, she wouldn't stay here long—not unless more people came and made the place amusing.

Some snow slid off the roof with a soft whooshing sound. Mrs. Boyle jumped. "No," she said out loud. "I shan't stay here long."

Somebody laughed—a faint, high chuckle. She turned her head sharply. Young Wren was standing in the doorway looking at her with that curious expression of his.

"No," he said. "I don't suppose you will."

Major Metcalf was helping Giles to shovel away snow from the back door. He was a good worker, and Giles was quite vociferous in his expressions of gratitude.

"Good exercise," said Major Metcalf. "Must get exercise every day. Got to keep fit, you know."

So the major was an exercise fiend. Giles had feared as much. It went with his demand for breakfast at half past seven.

As though reading Giles's thoughts, the major said, "Very good of your missus to cook me an early breakfast. Nice to get a new-laid egg, too."

Giles had risen himself before seven, owing to the exigencies of hotelkeeping. He and Molly had had boiled eggs and tea and had set to on the sitting-rooms. Everything was spick-and-span. Giles could not help thinking that if he had been a guest in his own establishment, nothing would have dragged him out of bed on a morning such as this until the last possible moment.

The major, however, had been up and breakfasted, and roamed about the house, apparently full of energy seeking an outlet.

Well, thought Giles, *there's plenty of snow to shovel.*

He threw a sideways glance at his companion. Not an easy man to place, really. Hard-bitten, well over middle age, something queerly watchful about the eyes. A man who was giving nothing away. Giles wondered why he had come to Monkswell Manor. Demobolized, probably, and no job to go to.

Mr. Paravicini came down late. He had coffee and a piece of toast—a frugal Continental breakfast.

He somewhat disconcerted Molly when she brought it to him by rising to his feet, bowing in an exaggerated manner, and exclaiming, "My charming hostess? I am right, am I not?"

Molly admitted rather shortly that he was right. She was in no mood for compliments at this hour.

"And why," she said, as she piled crockery recklessly

in the sink, "everybody has to have their breakfast at a different time— It's a bit hard."

She slung the plates into the rack and hurried upstairs to deal with the beds. She could expect no assistance from Giles this morning. He had to clear a way to the boiler house and to the henhouse.

Molly did the beds at top speed and admittedly in the most slovenly manner, smoothing sheets and pulling them up as fast as she could.

She was at work on the baths when the telephone rang.

Molly first cursed at being interrupted, then felt a slight feeling of relief that the telephone at least was still in action, as she ran down to answer it.

She arrived in the library a little breathless and lifted the receiver.

"Yes?"

A hearty voice with a slight but pleasant country burr asked, "Is that Monkswell Manor?"

"Monkswell Manor Guest House."

"Can I speak to Commander Davis, Please?"

"I'm afraid he can't come to the telephone just now," said Molly. "This is Mrs. Davis. Who is speaking, please?"

"Superintendent Hogben, Berkshire Police."

Molly gave a slight gasp. She said, "Oh, yes—er—yes?"

"Mrs. Davis, rather an urgent matter has arisen. I don't wish to say very much over the telephone, but I have sent Detective Sergeant Trotter out to you, and he should be there any minute now."

"But he won't get here. We're snowed up—completely snowed up. The roads are impassable."

There was no break in the confidence of the voice at the other end.

"Trotter will get to you, all right," it said. "And please

impress upon your husband, Mrs. Davis, to listen very carefully to what Trotter has to tell you, and to follow his instructions implicitly. That's all."

"But, Superintendent Hogben, what—"

But there was a decisive click. Hogben had clearly said all he had to say and rung off. Molly waggled the telephone rest once or twice, then gave up. She turned as the door opened.

"Oh, Giles darling, there you are."

Giles had snow on his hair and a good deal of coal grime on his face. He looked hot.

"What is it, sweetheart? I've filled the coal scuttles and brought in the wood. I'll do the hens next and then have a look at the boiler. Is that right? What's the matter, Molly? You looked scared."

"Giles, it was the *police*."

"The police?" Giles sounded incredulous.

"Yes, they're sending out an inspector or a sergeant or something."

"But why? What have we done?"

"I don't know. Do you think it could be that two pounds of butter we had from Ireland?"

Giles was frowning. "I did remember to get the wireless license, didn't I?"

"Yes, it's in the desk. Giles, old Mrs. Bidlock gave me five of her coupons for that old tweed coat of mine. I suppose that's wrong—but *I* think it's perfectly fair. I'm a coat less so why shouldn't I have the coupons? Oh, dear, what else is there we've done?"

"I had a near shave with the car the other day. But it was definitely the other fellow's fault. Definitely."

"We must have done *something*," wailed Molly.

"The trouble is that practically everything one does nowadays is illegal," said Giles gloomily. "That's why one has a permanent feeling of guilt. Actually I expect it's something to do with running this place. Running a guest house is probably chock-full of snags we've never heard of."

"I thought drink was the only thing that mattered. We haven't given anyone anything to drink. Otherwise, why shouldn't we run our own house any way we please?"

"I know. It sounds all right. But as I say, everything's more or less forbidden nowadays."

"Oh, dear," sighed Molly. "I wish we'd never started. We're going to be snowed up for days, and everybody will be cross and they'll eat all our reserves of tins—"

"Cheer up, sweetheart," said Giles. "We're having a bad break at the moment, but it will pan out all right."

He kissed the top of her head rather absent-mindedly and, releasing her, said in a different voice, "You know, Molly, come to think of it, it must be something pretty serious to send a police sergeant trekking out here in all this." He waved a hand toward the snow outside. He said, "It must be something really *urgent*—"

As they stared at each other, the door opened, and Mrs. Boyle came in.

"Ah, here you are, Mr. Davis," said Mrs. Boyle. "Do you know the central heating in the drawing-room is practically stone-cold?"

"I'm sorry, Mrs. Boyle. We're rather short of coke and—"

Mrs. Boyle cut in ruthlessly. "I am paying seven guineas a week here—*seven* guineas. And I do *not* expect to freeze."

Giles flushed. He said shortly, "I'll go and stoke it up."

He went out of the room, and Mrs. Boyle turned to Molly.

"If you don't mind my saying so, Mrs. Davis, that is a very extraordinary young man you have staying here.

His manners—and his ties— And does he never brush his hair?"

"He's an extremely brilliant young architect," said Molly.

"I beg your pardon?"

"Christopher Wren is an architect and—"

"My dear young woman," snapped Mrs. Boyle, "I have naturally heard of Sir Christopher Wren. Of course he was an architect. He built St. Paul's. You young people seem to think that education came in with the Education Act."

"I meant this Wren. His name is Christopher. His parents called him that because they hoped he'd be an architect. And he is—or nearly—one, so it turned out all right."

"Humph," Mrs. Boyle snorted. "It sounds a very fishy story to me. I should make some inquiries about him if I were you. What do you know about him?"

"Just as much as I know about you, Mrs. Boyle—which is that both you and he are paying us seven guineas a week. That's really all that I need to know, isn't it? And all that concerns me. It doesn't matter to me whether I like my guests, or whether—" Molly looked very steadily at Mrs. Boyle—"or whether I don't."

Mrs. Boyle flushed angrily. "You are young and inexperienced and should welcome advice from someone more knowledgeable than yourself. And what about this queer foreigner? When did *he* arrive?"

"In the middle of the night."

"Indeed. Most peculiar. Not a very conventional hour."

"To turn away bona fide travelers would be against the law, Mrs. Boyle." Molly added sweetly, "You may not be aware of that."

"All I can say is that this Paravicini, or whatever he

calls himself, seems to me—"

"Beware, beware, dear lady. You talk of the devil and then—"

Mrs. Boyle jumped as though it had been indeed the devil who addressed her. Mr. Paravicini, who had minced quietly in without either of the two women noticing him, laughed and rubbed his hands together with a kind of elderly satanic glee.

"You startled me," said Mrs. Boyle. "I did not hear you come in."

"I come in on tiptoe, so," said Mr. Paravicini. "Nobody ever hears me come and go. That I find very amusing. Sometimes I overhear things. That, too, amuses me." He added softly, "But I do not forget what I hear."

Mrs. Boyle said rather feebly, "Indeed? I must get my knitting—I left it in the drawing-room."

She went out hurriedly. Molly stood looking at Mr. Paravicini with a puzzled expression. He approached her with a kind of hop and skip.

"My charming hostess looks upset." Before she could prevent it, he picked up her hand and kissed it. "What is it, dear lady?"

Molly drew back a step. She was not sure that she liked Mr. Paravicini much. He was leering at her like an elderly satyr.

"Everything is rather difficult this morning," she said lightly. "Because of the snow."

"Yes." Mr. Paravicini turned his head round to look out of the window. "Snow makes everything very difficult, does it not? Or else it makes things very easy."

"I don't know what you mean."

"No," he said thoughtfully. "There is quite a lot that you do not know. I think, for one thing, that you do not know very much about running a guest house."

Molly's chin went up belligerently. "I daresay we don't. But we mean to make a go of it."

"Bravo, bravo."

"After all," Molly's voice betrayed slight anxiety, "I'm not such a very bad cook—"

"You are, without doubt, an enchanting cook," said Mr. Paravicini.

What a nuisance foreigners were, thought Molly.

Perhaps Mr. Paravicini read her thoughts. At all events his manner changed. He spoke quietly and quite seriously.

"May I give you a little word of warning, Mrs. Davis? You and your husband must not be too trusting, you know. Have you references with these guests of yours?"

"Is that usual?" Molly looked troubled. "I thought people just—just came."

"It is advisable always to know a little about the people who sleep under your roof." He leaned forward and tapped her on the shoulder in a minatory kind of way. "Take myself, for example. I turn up in the middle of the night. My car, I say, is overturned in a snowdrift. What do you know of me? Nothing at all. Perhaps you know nothing, either, of your other guests."

"Mrs. Boyle—" began Molly, but stopped as that lady herself re-entered the room, knitting in hand.

"The drawing-room is too cold. I shall sit in here." She marched toward the fireplace.

Mr. Paravicini pirouetted swiftly ahead of her. "Allow me to poke the fire for you."

Molly was struck, as she had been the night before, by the youthful jauntiness of his step. She had noticed that he always seemed careful to keep his back to the light, and now, as he knelt, poking the fire, she thought she saw the reason for it. Mr. Paravicini's face was cleverly but decidedly "made up."

So the old idiot tried to make himself look younger than he was, did he? Well, he didn't succeed. He looked all his age and more. Only the youthful walk was incongruous. Perhaps that, too, had been carefully counterfeited.

She was brought back from speculation to the disagreeable realities by the brisk entrance of Major Metcalf.

"Mrs. Davis. I'm afraid the pipes of the —er—" he lowered his voice modestly, "downstairs cloakroom are frozen."

"Oh, dear," groaned Molly. "What an awful day. First the police and then the pipes."

Mr. Paravicini dropped the poker into the grate with a clatter. Mrs. Boyle stopped knitting. Molly, looking at Major Metcalf, was puzzled by his sudden stiff immobility and by the indescribable expression on his face. It was an expression she could not place. It was as though all emotion had been drained out of it, leaving something carved out of wood behind.

He said in a short, staccato voice, *"Police,* did you say?"

She was conscious that behind the stiff immobility of his demeanor, some violent emotion was at work. It might have been fear or alertness or excitement—but there was *something. This man,* she said to herself, *could be dangerous.*

He said again, and this time his voice was just mildly curious, "What's that about the police?"

"They rang up," said Molly. "Just now. To say they're sending a sergeant out here." She looked toward the window. "But I shouldn't think he'll ever get here," she said hopefully.

"Why are they sending the police here?" He took a step nearer to her, but before she could reply the door opened, and Giles came in.

"This ruddy coke's more than half stones," he said angrily. Then he added sharply, "Is anything the matter?"

Major Metcalf turned to him. "I hear the police are coming out here," he said. "Why?"

"Oh, that's all right," said Giles. "No one can ever get through in this. Why, the drifts are five feet deep. The road's all banked up. Nobody will get here today."

And at that moment there came distinctly three loud taps on the window.

It startled them all. For a moment or two they did not locate the sound. It came with the emphasis and menace of a ghostly warning. And then, with a cry, Molly pointed to the French window. A man was standing there tapping on the pane, and the mystery of his arrival was explained by the fact that he wore skis.

With an exclamation, Giles crossed the room, fumbled with the catch, and threw open the French window.

"Thank you, sir," said the new arrival. He had a slightly common, cheerful voice and a well-bronzed face.

"Detective Sergeant Trotter," he announced himself.

Mrs. Boyle peered at him over her knitting with disfavor. "You can't be a sergeant," she said disapprovingly. "You're too young."

The young man, who was indeed very young, looked affronted at this criticism and said in a slightly annoyed tone, "I'm not quite as young as I look, madam."

His eye roved over the group and picked out Giles.

"Are you Mr. Davis? Can I get these skis off and stow them somewhere?"

"Of course, come with me."

Mrs. Boyle said acidly as the door to the hall closed behind them, "I suppose that's what we pay our police force for, nowadays, to go round enjoying themselves at winter sports."

Paravicini had come close to Molly. There was quite a hiss in his voice as he said in a quick, low voice, "Why did you send for the police, Mrs. Davis?"

She recoiled a little before the steady malignity of his glance. This was a new Mr. Paravicini. For a moment she felt afraid. She said helplessly, "But I didn't. I didn't."

And then Christopher Wren came excitedly through the door, saying in a high penetrating whisper, "Who's that man in the hall? Where did he come from? So terribly hearty and all over snow."

Mrs. Boyle's voice boomed out over the click of her knitting-needles. "You may believe it or not, but that man is a policeman. A policeman—skiing!"

The final disruption of the lower classes had come, so her manner seemed to say.

Major Metcalf murmured to Molly, "Excuse me, Mrs. Davis, but may I use your telephone?"

"Of course, Major Metcalf."

He went over to the instrument, just as Christopher Wren said shrilly, "He's very handsome, don't you think so? I always think policemen are terribly attractive."

"Hullo, hullo—" Major Metcalf was rattling the telephone irritably. He turned to Molly. "Mrs. Davis, this telephone is dead, quite dead."

"It was all right just now. I—"

She was interrupted. Christopher Wren was laughing, a high, shrill, almost hysterical laugh. "So we're quite cut off now. Quite cut off. That's funny, isn't it?"

"I don't see anything to laugh at," said Major Metcalf stiffly.

"No, indeed," said Mrs. Boyle.

Christopher was still in fits of laughter. "It's a private joke of my own," he said. "*Hsh,*" he put his finger to his lips, "the sleuth is coming."

Giles came in with Sergeant Trotter. The latter had got rid of his skis and brushed off the snow and was holding in his hand a large notebook and pencil. He brought an atmosphere of unhurried judicial procedure with him.

"Molly," said Giles, "Sergeant Trotter wants a word with us alone."

Molly followed them both out of the room.

"We'll go in the study," Giles said.

They went into the small room at the back of the hall which was dignified by that name. Sergeant Trotter closed the door carefully behind him.

"What have we done, Sergeant?" Molly demanded plaintively.

"Done?" Sergeant Trotter stared at her. Then he smiled broadly. "Oh," he said. "It's nothing of that kind, madam. I'm sorry if there's been a misapprehension of any kind. No, Mrs. Davis, it's something quite different. It's more a matter of police protection, if you understand me."

Not understanding him in the least, they both looked at him inquiringly.

Sergeant Trotter went on fluently. "It relates to the death of Mrs. Lyon, Mrs. Maureen Lyon, who was murdered in London two days ago. You may have read about the case."

"Yes," said Molly.

"The first thing I want to know is if you were acquainted with this Mrs. Lyon?"

"Never heard of her," said Giles, and Molly murmured concurrence.

"Well, that's rather what we expected. But as a matter of fact Lyon wasn't the murdered woman's real name. She had a police record, and her fingerprints were on file, so we were able to identify her without any difficulty.

Her real name was Gregg; Maureen Gregg. Her late husband, John Gregg, was a farmer who resided at Longridge Farm not very far from here. You may have heard of the Longridge Farm case."

The room was very still. Only one sound broke the stillness, a soft, unexpected *prop* as snow slithered off the roof and fell to the ground outside. It was a secret, almost sinister sound.

Trotter went on. "Three evacuee children were billeted on the Greggs at Longridge Farm in 1940. One of those children subsequently died as the result of criminal neglect and ill-treatment. The case made quite a sensation, and the Greggs were both sentenced to terms of imprisonment. Gregg escaped on his way to prison, he stole a car and had a crash while trying to evade the police. He was killed outright. Mrs. Gregg served her sentence and was released two months ago."

"And now she's been murdered," said Giles. "Who do they think did it?"

But Sergeant Trotter was not to be hurried. "You remember the case, sir?" he asked.

Giles shook his head. "In 1940 I was a midshipman serving in the Mediterranean."

Trotter transferred his glance to Molly.

"I—I do remember hearing about it, I think," said Molly rather breathlessly. "But why do you come to us? What have we to do with it?"

"It's a question of your being in danger, Mrs. Davis!"

"Danger?" Giles spoke incredulously.

"It's like this, sir. A notebook was picked up near the scene of the crime. In it were written two addresses. The first was Seventy-Four Culver Street."

"Where the woman was murdered?" Molly put in.

"Yes, Mrs. Davis. The other address was Monkswell Manor."

"What?" Molly's tone was incredulous. "But how extraordinary."

"Yes. That's why Superintendent Hogben thought it imperative to find out if you knew of any connection between you, or between this house, and the Longridge Farm case."

"There's nothing—absolutely nothing," said Giles. "It must be some coincidence."

Sergeant Trotter said gently, "Superintendent Hogben dosen't think it is a coincidence. He'd have come himself if it had been at all possible. Under the weather conditions, and as I'm an expert skier, he sent me with instructions to get full particulars of everyone in this house, to report back to him by phone, and to take all measures I thought expedient for the safety of the household."

Giles said sharply, "Safety? Good Lord, man, you don't think somebody is going to be killed *here*?"

Trotter said apologetically, "I didn't want to upset the lady, but yes, that is just what Superintendent Hogben does think."

"But what earthly reason could there be—"

Giles broke off, and Trotter said, "That's just what I'm here to find out."

"But the whole thing's *crazy*."

"Yes, sir. But it's because it's crazy that it's dangerous."

Molly said, "There's something more you haven't told us yet, isn't there, Sergeant?"

"Yes, madam. At the top of the page in the notebook was written, 'Three Blind Mice.' Pinned to the dead woman's body was a paper with 'This is the first' written on it. And below it a drawing of *three mice* and a bar of music. The music was the tune of the nursery rhyme 'Three Blind Mice.' "

Molly sang softly:

> *"Three Blind Mice,*
> *See how they run.*
> *They all ran after the farmer's wife!*
> *She—"*

She broke off. "Oh, it's horrible—*horrible*. There were three children, weren't there?"

"Yes, Mrs. Davis. A boy of fifteen, a girl of fourteen, and the boy of twelve who died."

"What happened to the others?"

"The girl was, I believe, adopted by someone. We haven't been able to trace her. The boy would be just on twenty-three now. We've lost track of him. He was said to have always been a bit—queer. He joined up in the army at eighteen. Later he deserted. Since then he's disappeared. The army psychiatrist says definitely that he's not normal."

"You think that it was he who killed Mrs. Lyon?" Giles asked. "And that he's a homicidal maniac and may turn up here for some unknown reason?"

"We think that there must be a connection between someone here and the Longridge Farm business. Once we can establish what that connection is, we will be forearmed. Now you state, sir, that you yourself have no connection with that case. The same goes for you, Mrs. Davis?"

"I—oh, yes—yes."

"Perhaps you will tell me exactly who else there is in the house?"

They gave him the names. Mrs. Boyle. Major Metcalf. Mr. Christopher Wren. Mr. Paravicini. He wrote them down in his notebook.

"Servants?"

"We haven't any servants," said Molly. "And that reminds me, I must go and put the potatoes on."

She left the study abruptly.

Trotter turned to Giles. "What do you know about these people, sir?"

"I— We—" Giles paused. Then he said quietly, "Really, we don't know anything about them, Sergeant Trotter. Mrs. Boyle wrote from a Bournemouth hotel. Major Metcalf from Leamington, Mr. Wren from a private hotel in South Kensington. Mr. Paravicini just turned up out of the blue—or rather out of the white—his car overturned in a snowdrift near here. Still, I suppose they'll have identity cards, ration books, that sort of thing?"

"I shall go into all that, of course."

"In a way it's lucky that the weather is so awful," said Giles. "The murderer can't very well turn up in this, can he?"

"Perhaps he doesn't need to, Mr. Davis."

"What do you mean?"

Sergeant Trotter hesitated for a moment and then he said, "You've got to consider, sir, that *he may be here already.*"

Giles stared at him.

"What do you mean?"

"Mrs. Gregg was killed two days ago. *All your visitors here have arrived since then, Mr. Davis.*"

"Yes, but they'd booked beforehand—some time beforehand—except for Paravicini."

Sergeant Trotter sighed. His voice sounded tired. "These crimes were planned in advance."

"Crimes? But only one crime has happened yet. Why are you sure that there will be another?"

"That it will happen—no. I hope to prevent that. That it will be attempted, yes."

"But then—if you're right," Giles spoke excitedly, "there's only one person it could be. There's only one person who's the right age. *Christopher Wren!*"

Sergeant Trotter had joined Molly in the kitchen.

"I'd be glad, Mrs. Davis, if you would come with me to the library. I want to make a general statement to everyone. Mr. Davis has kindly gone to prepare the way—"

"All right—just let me finish these potatoes. Sometimes I wish Sir Walter Raleigh had never discovered the beastly things."

Sergeant Trotter preserved a disapproving silence. Molly said apologetically, "I can't really believe it, you see— It's so fantastic—"

"It isn't fantastic, Mrs. Davis— It's just plain *facts*."

"You have a description of the man?" Molly asked curiously.

"Medium height, slight build, wore a dark overcoat and a light hat, spoke in a whisper, his face was hidden by a muffler. You see—that might be anybody." He paused and added, "There are three dark overcoats and light hats hanging up in your hall here, Mrs. Davis."

"I don't think any of these people came from London."

"Didn't they, Mrs. Davis?" With a swift movement Sergeant Trotter moved to the dresser and picked up a newspaper.

"The *Evening Standard* of February 19th. Two days ago. *Someone* brought that paper here, Mrs. Davis."

"But how extraordinary." Molly stared, some faint chord of memory stirred. "Where can that paper have come from?"

"You mustn't take people always at their face value, Mrs. Davis. You don't really know anything about these people you have admitted to your house." He added, "I take it you and Mr. Davis are new to the guest-house business?"

"Yes, we are," Molly admitted. She felt suddenly young, foolish, and childish.

"You haven't been married long, perhaps, either?"

"Just a year." She blushed slightly. "It was all rather sudden."

"Love at first sight," said Sergeant Trotter sympathetically.

Molly felt quite unable to snub him. "Yes," she said, and added in a burst of confidence, "we'd only known each other a fortnight."

Her thoughts went back over those fourteen days of whirlwind courtship. There hadn't been any doubts—they had both known. In a worrying, nerve-racked world, they had found the miracle of each other. A little smile came to her lips.

She came back to the present to find Sergeant Trotter eying her indulgently.

"Your husband doesn't come from these parts, does he?"

"No," said Molly vaguely. "He comes from Lincolnshire."

She knew very little of Giles's childhood and upbringing. His parents were dead, and he always avoided talking about his early days. He had had, she fancied, an unhappy childhood.

"You're both very young, if I may say so, to run a place of this kind," said Sergeant Trotter.

"Oh, I don't know. I'm twenty-two and—"

She broke off as the door opened and Giles came in.

"Everything's all set. I've given them a rough outline," he said. "I hope that's all right, Sergeant?"

"Saves time," said Trotter. "Are you ready, Mrs. Davis?"

Four voices spoke at once as Sergeant Trotter entered the library.

Highest and shrillest was that of Christopher Wren declaring that this was too, too thrilling and he wasn't going to sleep a wink tonight, and please, *please* could we have all the gory details?

A kind of double-bass accompaniment came from Mrs. Boyle. "Absolute outrage—sheer incompetence—police have no business to let murderers go roaming about the countryside."

Mr. Paravicini was eloquent chiefly with his hands. His gesticulations were more eloquent than his words, which were drowned by Mrs. Boyle's double bass. Major Metcalf could be heard in an occasional short staccato bark. He was asking for facts.

Trotter waited a moment or two, then he held up an authoritative hand and, rather surprisingly, there was silence.

"Thank you," he said. "Now, Mr. Davis has given you an outline of why I'm here. I want to know one thing, and one thing only, and I want to know it quick. *Which of you has some connection with the Longridge Farm case?*"

The silence was unbroken. Four blank faces looked at Sergeant Trotter. The emotions of a few moments back—excitement, indignation, hysteria, inquiry, were wiped away as a sponge wipes out the chalk marks on a slate.

Sergeant Trotter spoke again, more urgently. "Please understand me. One of you, we have reason to believe, is in danger—deadly danger. *I have got to know which one of you it is!*"

And still no one spoke or moved.

Something like anger came into Trotter's voice. "Very well—I'll ask you one by one. Mr. Paravicini?"

A very faint smile flickered across Mr. Paravicini's face. He raised his hands in a protesting foreign gesture.

"But I am a stranger in these parts, Inspector. I know nothing, but nothing, of these local affairs of bygone years."

Trotter wasted no time. He snapped out, "Mrs. Boyle?"

"Really I don't see why—I mean—why should *I* have anything to do with such a distressing business?"

"Mr. Wren?"

Christopher said shrilly, "I was a mere child at the time. I don't remember even *hearing* about it."

"Major Metcalf?"

The Major said abruptly, "Read about it in the papers. I was stationed at Edinburgh at the time."

"That's all you have to say—any of you?"

Silence again.

Trotter gave an exasperated sigh. "If one of you gets murdered," he said, "you'll only have yourself to blame." He turned abruptly and went out of the room.

"My dears," said Christopher. "How *melodramatic!*" He added, "He's very handsome, isn't he? I do admire the police. So stern and hard-boiled. Quite a thrill, this whole business. 'Three Blind Mice.' How does the tune go?"

He whistled the air softly, and Molly cried out involuntarily, *"Don't!"*

He whirled round on her and laughed. "But, darling," he said, "it's my *signature* tune. I've never been taken for a murderer before and I'm getting a tremendous kick out of it!"

"Melodramatic rubbish," said Mrs. Boyle. "I don't believe a word of it."

Christopher's light eyes danced with an impish mischief. "But just wait, Mrs. Boyle," he lowered his voice, "till I creep up behind you and you feel my hands round your throat."

Molly flinched.

Giles said angrily, "You're upsetting my wife, Wren. It's a damned poor joke, anyway."

"It's no joking matter," said Metcalf.

"Oh, but it is," said Christopher. "That's just what it is—a madman's joke. That's what makes it so deliciously *macabre.*"

He looked round at them and laughed again. "If you could just see your faces," he said.

Then he went swiftly out of the room.

Mrs. Boyle recovered first. "A singularly ill-mannered and neurotic young man," she said. "Probably a conscientious objector."

"He tells me he was buried during an air raid for forty-eight hours before being dug out," said Major Metcalf. "That accounts for a good deal, I daresay."

"People have so many excuses for giving way to nerves," said Mrs. Boyle acidly. "I'm sure I went through as much as anybody in the war, and *my* nerves are all right."

"Perhaps that's just as well for you, Mrs. Boyle," said Metcalf.

"What do you mean?"

Major Metcalf said quietly, "I think you were actually the billeting officer for this district in 1940, Mrs. Boyle." He looked at Molly who gave a grave nod. "That is so, isn't it?"

An angry flush appeared on Mrs. Boyle's face. "What of it?" she demanded.

Metcalf said gravely, *"You* were responsible for sending three children to Longridge Farm."

"Really, Major Metcalf, I don't see how I can be held responsible for what happened. The Farm people seemed very nice and were most anxious to have the children. I don't see that I was to blame in any way—or that I can be held responsible—" Her voice trailed off.

Giles said sharply, "Why didn't you tell Sergeant Trotter this?"

"No business of the police," snapped Mrs. Boyle. "I

can look after myself."

Major Metcalf said quietly, "You'd better watch out."
Then he, too, left the room.

Molly murmured, "Of course, you *were* the billeting officer. I remember."

"Molly, did you know?" Giles stared at her.

"You had the big house on the common, didn't you?"

"Requisitioned," said Mrs. Boyle. "And completely ruined," she added bitterly. *"Devastated.* Iniquitous."

Then, very softly, Mr. Paravicini began to laugh. He threw his head back and laughed without restraint.

"You must forgive me," he gasped. "But, indeed, I find all this most amusing. I enjoy myself—yes, I enjoy myself greatly."

Sergeant Trotter re-entered the room at that moment. He threw a glance of disapproval at Mr. Paravicini. "I'm glad," he said acidly, "that everyone finds this so funny."

"I apologize, my dear Inspector. I do apologize. I am spoiling the effect of your solemn warning."

Sergeant Trotter shrugged his shoulders. "I've done my best to make the position clear," he said. "And I'm not an inspector. I'm only a sergeant. I'd like to use the telephone, please, Mrs. Davis."

"I abase myself," said Mr. Paravicini. "I creep away."

Far from creeping, he left the room with that jaunty and youthful step that Molly had noticed before.

"He's an odd fish," said Giles.

"Criminal type," said Trotter. "Wouldn't trust him a yard."

"Oh," said Molly. "You think *he*—but he's far too old— Or is he old at all? He uses make-up—quite a lot of it. And his walk is young. Perhaps he's made up to *look* old. Sergeant Trotter, do you think—"

Sergeant Trotter snubbed her severely. "We shan't get anywhere with unprofitable speculation, Mrs. Davis," he said. "I must report to Superintendent Hogben."

He crossed to the telephone.

"But you can't," said Molly. "The telephone's dead."

"What?" Trotter swung round.

The sharp alarm in his voice impressed them all. "Dead? Since when?"

"Major Metcalf tried it just before you came."

"But it was all right before that. You got Superintendent Hogben's message?"

"Yes. I suppose—since ten—the line's down—with the snow."

But Trotter's face remained grave. "I wonder," he said. "It may have been—cut."

Molly stared. "You think so?"

"I'm going to make sure."

He hurried out of the room. Giles hesitated, then went after him.

Molly exclaimed, "Good heavens! Nearly lunch time, I must get on—or we'll have nothing to eat."

As she rushed from the room, Mrs. Boyle muttered, "Incompetent chit! What a place. *I* shan't pay seven guineas for *this* kind of thing."

Sergeant Trotter bent down, following the wires. He asked Giles, "Is there an extension?"

"Yes, in our bedroom upstairs. Shall I go up and see there?"

"If you please."

Trotter opened the window and leaned out, brushing snow from the sill. Giles hurried up the stairs.

Mr. Paravicini was in the big drawing-room. He went across to the grand piano and opened it. Sitting on the music stool, he picked out a tune softly with one finger.

Three Blind Mice,
See how they run . . .

Christopher Wren was in his bedroom. He moved about it, whistling briskly. Suddenly the whistle wavered and died. He sat down on the edge of the bed. He buried his face in his hands and began to sob. He murmured childishly, "I can't go on."

Then his mood changed. He stood up, squared his shoulders. "I've got to go on," he said. "I've got to go through with it."

Giles stood by the telephone in his and Molly's room. He bent down toward the skirting. One of Molly's gloves lay there. He picked it up. A pink bus ticket dropped out of it. Giles stood looking down at it as it fluttered to the ground. Watching it, his face changed. It might have been a different man who walked slowly, as though in a dream, to the door, opened it, and stood a moment peering along the corridor toward the head of the stairs.

Molly finished the potatoes, threw them into the pot, and set the pot on the fire. She glanced into the oven. Everything was all set, going according to plan.

On the kitchen table was the two-day-old copy of the *Evening Standard.* She frowned as she looked at it. If she could only just *remember—*

Suddenly her hands went to her eyes. "Oh, no," said Molly. "Oh, *no!*"

Slowly she took her hands away. She looked round the kitchen like someone looking at a strange place. So warm and comfortable and spacious, with its faint savory smell of cooking.

"Oh, *no,*" she said again under her breath.

She moved slowly, like a sleepwalker, toward the door into the hall. She opened it. The house was silent except for someone whistling.

That tune—

Molly shivered and retreated. She waited a minute or two, glancing once more round the familiar kitchen. Yes, everything was in order and progressing. She went once more toward the kitchen door.

Major Metcalf came quietly down the back stairs. He waited a moment or two in the hall, then he opened the big cupboard under the stairs and peered in. Everything seemed quiet. Nobody about. As good a time as any to do what he had set out to do—

Mrs. Boyle, in the library, turned the knobs of the radio with some irritation.

Her first attempt had brought her into the middle of a talk on the origin and significance of nursery rhymes. The last thing she wanted to hear. Twirling impatiently, she was informed by a cultured voice: "The psychology of fear must be thoroughly understood. Say you are alone in a room. A door opens softly behind you—"

A door did open.

Mrs. Boyle, with a violent start, turned sharply. "Oh, it's you," she said with relief. "Idiotic programs they have on this thing. I can't find anything worth listening to!"

"I shouldn't bother to listen, Mrs. Boyle."

Mrs. Boyle snorted. "What else is there for me to do?" she demanded. "Shut up in a house with a possible murderer—not that I believe *that* melodramatic story for a moment—"

"Don't you, Mrs. Boyle?"

"Why—what do you mean—"

The belt of the raincoat was slipped round her neck so quickly that she hardly realized its significance. The knob of the radio amplifier was turned higher. The lecturer on the psychology of fear shouted his learned remarks into the room and drowned what incidental noises there were attendant on Mrs. Boyle's demise.

But there wasn't much noise.

The killer was too expert for that.

They were all huddled in the kitchen. On the gas cooker the potatoes bubbled merrily. The savory smell from the oven of steak and kidney pie was stronger than ever.

Four shaken people stared at each other, the fifth, Molly, white and shivering, sipped at the glass of whisky that the sixth, Sergeant Trotter, had forced her to drink.

Sergeant Trotter himself, his face set and angry, looked round at the assembled people. Just five minutes had elapsed since Molly's terrified screams had brought him and the others racing to the library.

"She'd only just been killed when you got to her, Mrs. Davis," he said. "Are you sure you didn't see or hear anybody as you came across the hall?"

"Whistling," said Molly faintly. "But that was earlier. I think—I'm not sure—I think I heard a door shut—softly, somewhere—just as I—as I—went into the library."

"Which door?"

"I don't know."

"Think, Mrs. Davis—try and *think*—upstairs—downstairs—right, left?"

"I don't *know,* I tell you," cried Molly. "I'm not even sure I heard anything."

"Can't you stop bullying her?" said Giles angrily. "Can't you see she's all in?"

"I'm investigating a murder, Mr. Davis—I beg your pardon—*Commander* Davis."

"I don't use my war rank, Sergeant."

"Quite so, sir." Trotter paused, as though he had made some subtle point. "As I say, I'm investigating a murder. Up to now nobody has taken this thing seriously. Mrs.

Boyle didn't. She held out on me with information. You all held out on me. Well, Mrs. Boyle is dead. Unless we get to the bottom of this—and quickly, mind, there may be another death."

"Another? Nonsense. Why?"

"Because," said Sergeant Trotter gravely, "there were three little blind mice."

Giles said incredulously, "A death for each of them? But there would have to be a connection—I mean another connection with the case."

"Yes, there would have to be that."

"But why another death *here?*"

"Because there were only two addresses in the notebook. There was only one possible victim at Seventy-Four Culver Street. She's dead. But at Monkswell Manor there is a wider field."

"Nonsense, Trotter. It would be a most unlikely coincidence that there should be *two* people brought here by chance, both of them with a share in the Longridge Farm case."

"Given certain circumstances, it wouldn't be so much of a coincidence. Think it out, Mr. Davis." He turned toward the others. "I've had your accounts of where you all were when Mrs. Boyle was killed. I'll check them over. You were in your room, Mr. Wren, when you heard Mrs. Davis scream?"

"Yes, Sergeant."

"Mr. Davis, you were upstairs in your bedroom examining the telephone extension there?"

"Yes," said Giles.

"Mr. Paravicini was in the drawing-room playing tunes on the piano. Nobody heard you, by the way, Mr. Paravicini?"

"I was playing very, very softly, Sergeant, just with one finger."

"What tune was it?"

" 'Three Blind Mice,' Sergeant." He smiled. "The same tune that Mr. Wren was whistling upstairs. The tune that's running through everybody's head."

"It's a horrid tune," said Molly.

"How about the telephone wire?" asked Metcalf. "Was it deliberately cut?"

"Yes, Major Metcalf. A section had been cut out just outside the dining-room window—I had just located the break when Mrs. Davis screamed."

"But it's crazy. How can he hope to get away with it?" demanded Christopher shrilly.

The sergeant measured him carefully with his eye.

"Perhaps he doesn't very much care about that," he said. "Or again, he may be quite sure he's too clever for us. Murderers get like that." He added, "We take a psychology course, you know, in our training. A schizophrenic's mentality is very interesting."

"Shall we cut out the long words?" said Giles.

"Certainly, Mr. Davis. Two six-letter words are all that concern us at the moment. One's 'murder' and the other's 'danger.' That's what we've got to concentrate upon. Now, Major Metcalf, let me be quite clear about your movements. You say you were in the *cellar*— Why?"

"Looking around," said the major. "I looked in that cupboard place under the stairs and then I noticed a door there and I opened it and saw a flight of steps, so I went down there. Nice cellars, you've got," he said to Giles. "Crypt of an old monastery, I should say."

"We're not engaged in antiquarian research, Major Metcalf. We're investigating a murder. Will you listen a moment, Mrs. Davis? I'll leave the kitchen door open." He went out; a door shut with a faint creak. "Is that what you heard, Mrs. Davis?" he asked as he reappeared in the open doorway.

"I—it does sound like it."

"That was the cupboard under the stairs. It could be, you know, that after killing Mrs. Boyle, the murderer, retreating across the hall, heard you coming out of the kitchen, and slipped into the cupboard, pulling the door to after him."

"Then his fingerprints will be on the inside of the cupboard," cried Christopher.

"Mine are there already," said Major Metcalf.

"Quite so," said Sergeant Trotter. "But we've a satisfactory explanation for those, haven't we?" he added smoothly.

"Look here, Sergeant," said Giles, "admittedly you're in charge of this affair. But this is my house, and in a certain degree I feel responsible for the people staying in it. Oughtn't we to take precautionary measures?"

"Such as, Mr. Davis?"

"Well, to be frank, putting under restraint the person who seems pretty clearly indicated as the chief suspect."

He looked straight at Christopher Wren.

Christopher Wren sprang forward, his voice rose, shrill and hysterical. "It's not true! It's not *true!* You're all against me. Everyone's always against me. You're going to frame me for this. It's persecution—persecution—"

"Steady on, lad," said Major Metcalf.

"It's all right, Chris." Molly came forward. She put her hand on his arm. "Nobody's against you. Tell him it's all right," she said to Sergeant Trotter.

"We don't frame people," said Sergeant Trotter.

"Tell him you're not going to arrest him."

"I'm not going to arrest anyone. To do that, I need evidence. There's no evidence—at present."

Giles cried out, "I think you're crazy, Molly. And you, too, Sergeant. There's only one person who fits the bill, and—"

"Wait, Giles, wait—" Molly broke in. "Oh, do be quiet. Sergeant Trotter, can I—can I speak to you a minute?"

"I'm staying," said Giles.

"No, Giles, you, too, please."

Giles's face grew as dark as thunder. He said, "I don't know what's come over you, Molly."

He followed the others out of the room, banging the door behind him.

"Yes, Mrs. Davis, what is it?"

"Sergeant Trotter, when you told us about the Longridge Farm case, you seemed to think that it must be the eldest boy who is—responsible for all this. But you don't *know* that?"

"That's perfectly true, Mrs. Davis. But the probabilities lie that way—mental instability, desertion from the army, psychiatrist's report."

"Oh, I know, and therefore it all seems to point to Christopher. But I don't believe it *is* Christopher. There must be other—possibilities. Hadn't those three children any relations—parents, for instance?"

"Yes. The mother was dead. But the father was serving abroad."

"Well, what about him? Where is *he* now?"

"We've no information. He obtained his demobilization papers last year."

"And if the son was mentally unstable, the father may have been, too."

"That is so."

"So the murderer may be middle-aged or old. Major Metcalf, remember, was frightfully upset when I told him the police had rung up. He really *was*."

Sergeant Trotter said quietly, "Please believe me, Mrs. Davis, I've had all the possibilities in mind since the beginning. The boy, Jim—the father—even the sister. It *could* have been a woman, you know. I haven't over-

looked anything. I may be pretty sure in my own mind—
but I don't *know*—yet. It's very hard really to know
about anything or anyone—especially in these days. You'd
be surprised what we see in the police force. With marriages, especially. Hasty marriages—war marriages.
There's no background, you see. No families or relations
to meet. People accept each other's word. Fellow says
he's a fighter pilot or an army major—the girl believes
him implicitly. Sometimes she doesn't find out for a year
or two that he's an absconding bank clerk with a wife
and family, or an army—deserter."

He paused and went on.

"I know quite well what's in your mind, Mrs. Davis.
There's just one thing I'd like to say to you. *The murderer's enjoying himself*. That's the one thing I'm quite sure
of."

He went toward the door.

Molly stood very straight and still, a red flush burning
in her cheeks. After standing rigid for a moment or two,
she moved slowly toward the stove, knelt down, and
opened the oven door. A savory, familiar smell came
toward her. Her heart lightened. It was as though suddenly she had been wafted back into the dear, familiar
world of everyday things. Cooking, housework, home-
making, ordinary prosaic living.

So, from time immemorial women had cooked food
for their men. The world of danger—of madness, receded.
Woman, in her kitchen, was safe—eternally safe.

The kitchen door opened. She turned her head as
Christopher Wren entered. He was a little breathless.

"My dear," he said. "*Such* ructions! Somebody's stolen
the sergeant's skis!"

"The sergeant's skis? But why should anyone want to
do that?"

"I really can't imagine. I mean, if the sergeant decided

to go away and leave us, I should imagine that the murderer would be only too pleased. I mean, it really doesn't make *sense*, does it?"

"Giles put them in the cupboard under the stairs."

"Well, they're not there now. Intriguing, isn't it?" He laughed gleefully. "The sergeant's awfully angry about it. Snapping like a turtle. He's been pitching into poor Major Metcalf. The old boy sticks to it that he didn't notice whether they were there or not when he looked into the cupboard just before Mrs. Boyle was murdered. Trotter says he *must* have noticed. If you ask me," Christopher lowered his voice and leaned forward, "this business is beginning to get Trotter down."

"It's getting us all down," said Molly.

"Not me. I find it most stimulating. It's all so delightfully unreal."

Molly said sharply, "You wouldn't say that if—if you'd been the one to find her. Mrs. Boyle, I mean. I keep thinking of it— I can't forget it. Her face—all swollen and purple—"

She shivered. Christopher came across to her. He put a hand on her shoulder.

"I know. I'm an idiot. I'm sorry. I didn't think."

A dry sob rose in Molly's throat. "It seemed all right just now—cooking—the kitchen," she spoke confusedly, incoherently. "And then suddenly—it was all back again —like a nightmare."

There was a curious expression on Christopher Wren's face as he stood there looking down on her bent head.

"I see," he said. "I see." He moved away. "Well, I'd better clear out and—not interrupt you."

Molly cried, "Don't go!" just as his hand was on the door handle.

He turned round, looking at her questioningly. Then he came slowly back.

"Do you really mean that?"

"Mean what?"

"You definitely don't want me to—go?"

"No, I tell you. I don't want to be alone. I'm afraid to be alone."

Christopher sat down by the table. Molly bent to the oven, lifted the pie to a higher shelf, shut the oven door, and came and joined him.

"That's very interesting," said Christopher in a level voice.

"What is?"

"That you're not afraid to be—alone with me. You're not, are you?"

She shook her head. "No, I'm not."

"Why aren't you afraid, Molly?"

"I don't know—I'm not."

"And yet I'm the only person who—fits the bill. One murderer as per schedule."

"No," said Molly. "There are—other possibilities. I've been talking to Sergeant Trotter about them."

"Did he agree with you?"

"He didn't disagree," said Molly slowly.

Certain words sounded over and over again in her head. Especially that last phrase: *I know exactly what's in your mind, Mrs. Davis.* But did he? Could he possibly know? He had said, too, that the murderer was enjoying himself. Was that true?

She said to Christopher, "*You're* not exactly enjoying yourself, are you? In spite of what you said just now."

"Good God, no," said Christopher, staring. "What a very odd thing to say."

"Oh, I didn't say it. Sergeant Trotter did. I hate that man! He—he puts things into your head—things that aren't true—that can't possibly be true."

She put her hands to her head, covering her eyes with

them. Very gently Christopher took those hands away.

"Look here, Molly," he said, "what is all this?"

She let him force her gently into a chair by the kitchen table. His manner was no longer hysterical or childish.

"What's the matter, Molly?" he said.

Molly looked at him—a long appraising glance. She asked irrelevantly, "How long have I known you, Christopher? Two days?"

"Just about. You're thinking, aren't you, that though it's such a short time, we seem to know each other rather well."

"Yes—it's odd, isn't it?"

"Oh, I don't know. There's a kind of sympathy between us. Possibly because we've both—been up against it."

It was not a question. It was a statement. Molly let it pass. She said very quietly, and again it was a statement rather than a question, "Your name isn't really Christopher Wren, is it."

"No."

"Why did you—"

"Choose that? Oh, it seemed rather a pleasant whimsy. They used to jeer at me and call me Christopher Robin at school. Robin—Wren—association of ideas, I suppose."

"What's your real name?"

Christopher said quietly, "I don't think we'll go into that. It wouldn't mean anything to you. I'm not an architect. Actually, I'm a deserter from the army."

Just for a moment swift alarm leaped into Molly's eyes.

Christopher saw it. "Yes," he said. "Just like our unknown murderer. I told you I was the only one the specification fitted."

"Don't be stupid," said Molly. "I told you I didn't believe you were the murderer. Go on—tell me about yourself. What made you desert—nerves?"

"Being afraid, you mean? No, curiously enough, I wasn't afraid—not more than anyone else, that is to say. Actually I got a reputation for being rather cool under fire. No, it was something quite different. It was—my mother."

"Your mother?"

"Yes—you see, she was killed—in an air raid. Buried. They—they had to dig her out. I don't know what happened to me when I heard about it—I suppose I went a little mad. I thought, you see, it happened to *me*. I felt I had to get home quickly and—and dig myself out—I can't explain—it was all confused." He lowered his head to his hands and spoke in a muffled voice. "I wandered about a long time, looking for her—or for myself—I don't know which. And then, when my mind cleared up, I was afraid to go back—or to report—I knew I could never explain. Since then, I've just been—nothing."

He stared at her, his young face hollow with despair.

"You mustn't feel like that," said Molly gently. "You can start again."

"Can one ever do that?"

"Of course—you're quite young."

"Yes, but you see—I've come to the end."

"No," said Molly. "You haven't come to the end, you only think you have. I believe everyone has that feeling once, at least, in their lives—that it's the end, that they can't go on."

"You've had it, haven't you, Molly? You must have—to be able to speak like that."

"Yes."

"What was yours?"

"Mine was just what happened to a lot of people. I was engaged to a young fighter pilot—and he was killed."

"Wasn't there more to it than that?"

"I suppose there was. I'd had a nasty shock when I was younger. I came up against something that was rather cruel and beastly. It predisposed me to think that life was always—horrible. When Jack was killed it just confirmed my belief that the whole of life was cruel and treacherous."

"I know. And then, I suppose," said Christopher, watching her, "Giles came along."

"Yes." He saw the smile, tender, almost shy, that trembled on her mouth. "Giles came—everything felt right and safe and happy— Giles!"

The smile fled from her lips. Her face was suddenly stricken. She shivered as though with cold.

"What's the matter, Molly? What's frightening you? You *are* frightened, aren't you?"

She nodded.

"And it's something to do with Giles? Something he's said or done?"

"It's not Giles, really. It's that horrible man!"

"What horrible man?" Christopher was surprised. "Paravicini?"

"No, *no*. Sergeant Trotter."

"Sergeant Trotter?"

"Suggesting things—hinting things—putting horrible thoughts into my mind about Giles—thoughts that I didn't know were there. Oh, I hate him—I hate him."

Christopher's eyebrows rose in slow surprise. "Giles? *Giles!* Yes, of course, he and I are much of an age. He seems to me much older than I am—but I suppose he isn't, really. Yes, Giles might fit the bill equally well. But look here, Molly, that's all nonsense. Giles was down here with you the day that woman was killed in London."

Molly did not answer.

Christopher looked at her sharply. "Wasn't he here?"

Molly spoke breathlessly, the words coming out in an incoherent jumble. "He was out all day—in the car—he went over to the other side of the county about some wire netting in a sale there—at least that's what he said—that's what I thought—until—until—"

"Until what?"

Slowly Molly's hand reached out and traced the date of the *Evening Standard* that covered a portion of the kitchen table.

Christopher looked at it and said, "London edition, two days ago."

"It was in Giles's pocket when he came back. He—he must have been in London."

Christopher stared. He stared at the paper and he stared at Molly. He pursed up his lips and began to whistle, then checked himself abruptly. It wouldn't do to whistle that tune just now.

Choosing his words very carefully, and avoiding her eye, he said, "How much do you actually—know about Giles?"

"Don't," cried Molly. "Don't! That's just what that beast Trotter said—or hinted. That women often didn't know anything about the men that they married—especially in wartime. They—they just took the man's own account of himself."

"That's true enough, I suppose."

"Don't *you* say it, too! I can't bear it. It's just because we're all in such a state, so worked up. We'd—we'd believe *any* fantastic suggestion— It's not true! I—"

She stopped. The kitchen door had opened.

Giles came in. There was rather a grim look on his face. "Am I interrupting anything?" he asked.

Christopher slipped from the table. "I'm just taking a few cookery lessons," he said.

"Indeed? Well, look here, Wren, tête-à-têtes aren't

very healthy things at the present time. You keep out of the kitchen, do you hear?"

"Oh, but surely—"

"You keep away from my wife, Wren. She's not going to be the next victim."

"That," said Christopher, "is just what I'm worrying about."

If there was significance in the words, Giles did not apparently notice them. He merely turned a rather darker shade of brick-red. "I'll do the worrying," he said. "I can look after my own wife. Get the hell out of here."

Molly said in a clear voice, "Please go, Christopher. Yes—really."

Christopher moved slowly toward the door. "I shan't go very far," he said, and the words were addressed to Molly and held a very definite meaning.

"*Will* you get out of here?"

Christopher gave a high childish giggle. "Aye, aye, Commander," he said.

The door shut behind him. Giles turned on Molly.

"For God's sake, Molly, haven't you got *any* sense? Shut in here alone with a dangerous homicidal maniac!"

"He isn't the—" she changed her phrase quickly—"he isn't dangerous. Anyway, I'm on my guard. I can—look after myself."

Giles laughed unpleasantly. "So could Mrs. Boyle."

"Oh, Giles, *don't*."

"Sorry, my dear. But I'm het up. That wretched boy. What you see in him I can't imagine."

Molly said slowly, "I'm sorry for him."

"Sorry for a homicidal lunatic?"

Molly gave him a curious glance. "I could be sorry for a homicidal lunatic," she said.

"Calling him Christopher, too. Since when have you been on Christian-name terms?"

"Oh, Giles, don't be ridiculous. Everyone always uses Christian names nowadays. You know they do."

"Even after a couple of days? But perhaps it's more than that. Perhaps you knew Mr. Christopher Wren, the phony architect, before he came here? Perhaps you suggested to him that he *should* come here? Perhaps you cooked it all up between you?"

Molly stared at him. "Giles, have you gone out of your mind? What on earth are you suggesting?"

"I'm suggesting that Christopher Wren is an old friend, that you're on rather closer terms with him than you'd like me to know."

"Giles, you must be crazy!"

"I suppose you'll stick to it that you never saw him until he walked in here. Rather odd that he should come and stay in an out-of-the-way place like this, isn't it?"

"Is it any odder than that Major Metcalf and—and Mrs. Boyle should?"

"Yes—I think it is. I've always read that these murmuring loonies had a peculiar fascination for women. Looks as though it were true. How did you get to know him? How long has this been going on?"

"You're being absolutely absurd, Giles. I never saw Christopher Wren until he arrived here."

"You didn't go up to London to meet him two days ago and fix up to meet here as strangers?"

"You know perfectly well, Giles, I haven't been up to London for weeks."

"Haven't you? That's interesting." He fished a fur-lined glove out of his pocket and held it out. "That's one of the gloves you were wearing day before yesterday, isn't it? The day I was over at Sailham getting the netting."

"The day *you* were over at Sailham getting the netting," said Molly, eying him steadily. "Yes, I wore those gloves when I went out."

"You went to the village, you said. If you only went to the village, what is this doing inside that glove?"

Accusingly, he held out a pink bus ticket.

There was a moment's silence.

"You went to London," said Giles.

"All right," said Molly. Her chin shot up. "I went to London."

"To meet this chap Christopher Wren."

"No, not to meet Christopher."

"Then why did you go?"

"Just at the moment, Giles," said Molly, "I'm not going to tell you."

"Meaning you'll give yourself time to think up a good story!"

"I think," said Molly, "that I hate you!"

"I don't hate you," said Giles slowly. "But I almost wish I did. I simply feel that—I don't know you any more— I don't know anything about you."

"I feel the same," said Molly. "You—you're just a stranger. A man who lies to me—"

"When have I ever lied to you?"

Molly laughed. "Do you think I believed that story of yours about the wire netting? *You* were in London, too, that day."

"I suppose you saw me there," said Giles. "And you didn't trust me enough—"

"Trust you? I'll never trust anyone—ever—again."

Neither of them had noticed the soft opening of the kitchen door. Mr. Paravicini gave a little cough.

"So embarrassing," he murmured. "I do hope you young people are not both saying just a little more than you mean. One is so apt to in these lovers' quarrels."

"Lovers' quarrels," said Giles derisively. "That's good."

"Quite so, quite so," said Mr. Paravicini. "I know just

how you feel. I have been through all this myself when I was a younger man. But what I came to say was that the inspector person is simply insisting that we should all come into the drawing-room. It appears that he has an idea." Mr. Paravicini sniggered gently. "The police have a clue—yes, one hears that frequently. But an *idea?* I very much doubt it. A zealous and painstaking officer, no doubt, our Sergeant Trotter, but not, I think, over-endowed with brains."

"Go on, Giles," said Molly. "I've got the cooking to see to. Sergeant Trotter can do without me."

"Talking of cooking," said Mr. Paravicini, skipping nimbly across the kitchen to Molly's side, "have you ever tried chicken livers served on toast that has been thickly spread with *foie gras* and a very thin rasher of bacon smeared with French mustard?"

"One doesn't see much *foie gras* nowadays," said Giles. "Come on, Paravicini."

"Shall I stay and assist you, dear lady?"

"You come along to the drawing-room, Paravicini," said Giles.

Mr. Paravicini laughed softly.

"Your husband is afraid for you. Quite natural. He doesn't fancy the idea of leaving you alone with *me*. It is my sadistic tendencies he fears—not my dishonorable ones. I yield to force." He bowed gracefully and kissed the tips of his fingers.

Molly said uncomfortably, "Oh, Mr. Paravicini, I'm sure—"

Mr. Paravicini shook his head. He said to Giles, "You're very wise, young man. *Take no chances.* Can I prove to you—or to the inspector for that matter—that I am not a homicidal maniac? No, I cannot. Negatives are such difficult things to prove."

He hummed cheerfully.

Molly flinched. "Please, Mr. Paravicini—not that horrible tune."

" 'Three Blind Mice'—so it was! The tune has got into my head. Now I come to think of it, it is a gruesome little rhyme. Not a nice little rhyme at all. But children like gruesome things. You may have noticed that? That rhyme is very English—the bucolic, cruel English countryside. 'She cut off their tails with a carving-knife.' Of course a child would love that—I could tell you things about children—"

"Please don't," said Molly faintly. "I think you're cruel, too." Her voice rose hysterically. "You laugh and smile—you're like a cat playing with a mouse—playing—"

She began to laugh.

"Steady, Molly," said Giles. "Come along, we'll all go into the drawing-room together. Trotter will be getting impatient. Never mind the cooking. Murder is more important than food."

"I'm not sure that I agree with you," said Mr. Paravicini as he followed them with little skipping steps. "The condemned man ate a hearty breakfast—that's what they always say."

Christopher Wren joined them in the hall and received a scowl from Giles. He looked at Molly with a quick, anxious glance, but Molly, her head held high, walked looking straight ahead of her. They marched almost like a procession to the drawing-room door. Mr. Paravicini brought up the rear with his little skipping steps.

Sergeant Trotter and Major Metcalf were standing waiting in the drawing-room. The major was looking sulky. Sergeant Trotter was looking flushed and energetic.

"That's right," he said, as they entered. "I wanted you all together. I want to make a certain experiment—and for that I shall require your co-operation."

"Will it take long?" Molly asked. "I'm rather busy in the kitchen. After all, we've got to have a meal sometime."

"Yes," said Trotter. "I appreciate that, Mrs. Davis. But, if you'll excuse me, there are more important things than meals! Mrs. Boyle, for instance, won't need another meal."

"Really, Sergeant," said Major Metcalf, "that's an extraordinarily tactless way of putting things."

"I'm sorry, Major Metcalf, but I want everyone to co-operate in this."

"Have you found your skis, Sergeant Trotter?" asked Molly.

The young man reddened. "No, I have not, Mrs. Davis. But I may say I have a very shrewd suspicion who took them. And of why they were taken. I won't say any more at present."

"Please don't," begged Mr. Paravicini. "I always think explanations should be kept to the very end—that exciting last chapter, you know."

"This isn't a game, sir."

"Isn't it? Now there I think you're wrong. I think it *is* a game—to somebody."

"The *murderer* is enjoying himself," murmured Molly softly.

The others looked at her in astonishment. She flushed.

"I'm only quoting what Sergeant Trotter said to me."

Sergeant Trotter did not look too pleased. "It's all very well, Mr. Paravicini, mentioning last chapters and speaking as though this was a mystery thriller," he said. "This is real. This is happening."

"So long," said Christopher Wren, fingering his neck gingerly, "as it doesn't happen to me."

"Now, then," said Major Metcalf. "None of that,

young fellow. The sergeant here is going to tell us just what he wants us to do."

Sergeant Trotter cleared his throat. His voice became official.

"I took certain statements from you all a short time ago," he said. "Those statements related to your positions at the time when the murder of Mrs. Boyle occurred. Mr. Wren and Mr. Davis were in their separate bedrooms. Mrs. Davis was in the kitchen. Major Metcalf was in the cellar. Mr. Paravicini was here in this room—"

He paused and then went on.

"Those are the statements you made. I have no means of checking those statements. They may be true—they may not. To put it quite clearly—four of those statements are true—but *one of them is false*. Which one?"

He looked from face to face. Nobody spoke.

"Four of you are speaking the truth—one is lying. I have a plan that may help me to discover the liar. And if I discover that one of you lied to me—then I know who the murderer is."

Giles said sharply, "Not necessarily. Someone might have lied—for some other reason."

"I rather doubt that, Mr. Davis."

"But what's the idea, man? You've just said you've no means of checking these statements?"

"No, but supposing everyone was to go through these movements a second time."

"Bah," said Major Metcalf disparagingly. "Reconstruction of the crime. Foreign idea."

"Not a reconstruction of the *crime*, Major Metcalf. A reconstruction of the movements of apparently innocent persons."

"And what do you expect to learn from that?"

"You will forgive me if I don't make that clear just at the moment."

"You want," asked Molly, "a repeat performance?"

"More or less, Mrs. Davis."

There was a silence. It was, somehow, an uneasy silence.

It's a trap, thought Molly. *It's a trap—but I don't see how—*

You might have thought that there were five guilty people in the room, instead of one guilty and four innocent ones. One and all cast doubtful sideways glances at the assured, smiling young man who proposed this innocent-sounding maneuver.

Christopher burst out shrilly, "But I don't see—I simply can't see—what you can possibly hope to find out—just by making people do the same thing they did before. It seems to me just nonsense!"

"Does it, Mr. Wren?"

"Of course," said Giles slowly, "what you say goes, Sergeant. We'll co-operate. Are we all to do exactly what we did before?"

"The same actions will be performed, yes."

A faint ambiguity in the phrase made Major Metcalf look up sharply. Sergeant Trotter went on.

"Mr. Paravicini has told us that he sat at the piano and played a certain tune. Perhaps, Mr. Paravicini, you would kindly show us exactly what you did do?"

"But certainly, my dear Sergeant."

Mr. Paravicini skipped nimbly across the room to the grand piano and settled himself on the music stool.

"The maestro at the piano will play the signature tune to a murder," he said with a flourish.

He grinned, and with elaborate mannerisms he picked out with one finger the tune of "Three Blind Mice."

He's enjoying himself, thought Molly. *He's enjoying himself.*

In the big room the soft, muted notes had an almost

eerie effect.

"Thank you, Mr. Paravicini," said Sergeant Trotter. "That, I take it, is exactly how you played the tune on the—former occasion?"

"Yes, Sergeant, it is. I repeated it three times."

Sergeant Trotter turned to Molly. "Do you play the piano, Mrs. Davis?"

"Yes, Sergeant Trotter."

"Could you pick out the tune, as Mr. Paravicini has done, playing it in exactly the same manner?"

"Certainly I could."

"Then will you go and sit at the piano and be ready to do so when I give the signal?"

Molly looked slightly bewildered. Then she crossed slowly to the piano.

Mr. Paravicini rose from the piano stool with a shrill protest. "But, Sergeant, I understood that we were each to repeat our former roles. *I* was at the piano here."

"The same actions will be performed as on the former occasion—*but they will not necessarily be performed by the same people.*"

"I—don't see the point of that," said Giles.

"There *is* a point, Mr. Davis. It is a means of checking up on the original statements—and I may say of *one* statement in particular. Now, then, please. I will assign you your various stations. Mrs. Davis will be here—at the piano. Mr. Wren, will you kindly go to the kitchen? Just keep an eye on Mrs. Davis's dinner. Mr. Paravicini, will you go to Mr. Wren's bedroom? There you can exercise your musical talents by whistling 'Three Blind Mice' just as he did. Major Metcalf, will you go up to Mr. Davis's bedroom and examine the telephone there? And you, Mr. Davis, will you look into the cupboard in the hall and then go down to the cellar?"

There was a moment's silence. Then four people

moved slowly toward the door. Trotter followed them. He looked over his shoulder.

"Count up to fifty and then begin to play, Mrs. Davis," he said.

He followed the others out. Before the door closed Molly heard Mr. Paravicini's voice say shrilly, "I never knew the police were so fond of parlor games."

"Forty-eight, forty-nine, fifty."

Obediently, the counting finished, Molly began to play. Again the soft cruel little tune crept out into the big, echoing room.

> Three Blind Mice
> See how they run . . .

Molly felt her heart beating faster and faster. As Paravicini had said, it was a strangely haunting and gruesome little rhyme. It had that childish incomprehension of pity which is so terrifying if met with in an adult.

Very faintly, from upstairs, she could hear the same tune being whistled in the bedroom above—Paravicini enacting the part of Christopher Wren.

Suddenly, next door, the wireless went on in the library. Sergeant Trotter must have set that going. He himself, then, was playing the part of Mrs. Boyle.

But why? What was the point of it all? Where was the trap? For there was a trap, of that she was certain.

A draft of cold air blew across the back of her neck. She turned her head sharply. Surely the door had opened. Someone had come into the room— No, the room was empty. But suddenly she felt nervous—afraid. If someone *should* come in. Supposing Mr. Paravicini should skip round the door, should come skipping over to the piano, his long fingers twitching and twisting—

*"So you are playing your own funeral march, dear
lady, a happy thought—"* Nonsense—don't be stupid—
don't imagine things. Besides, you can hear him whistling
over your head. Just as he can hear you.

She almost took her fingers off the piano as the idea
came to her! Nobody *had* heard Mr. Paravicini playing.
Was that the trap? Was it, perhaps, possible that Mr.
Paravicini hadn't been playing at all? That he had been,
not in the drawing-room, but in the library. In the library, strangling Mrs. Boyle?

He had been annoyed, very annoyed, when Trotter
had arranged for her to play. He had laid stress on the
softness with which he had picked out the tune. Of
course, he had emphasized the softness in the hopes that
it would be too soft to be heard outside the room. Because if anyone heard it this time who hadn't heard it
last time—why then, Trotter would have got what he
wanted—*the person who had lied.*

The door of the drawing-room opened. Molly, strung
up to expect Paravicini, nearly screamed. But it was only
Sergeant Trotter who entered, just as she finished the
third repetition of the tune.

"Thank you, Mrs. Davis," he said.

He was looking extremely pleased with himself, and
his manner was brisk and confident.

Molly took her hands from the keys. "Have you got
what you wanted?" she asked.

"Yes, indeed." His voice was exultant. "I've got exactly what I wanted."

"Which? Who?"

"Don't you know, Mrs. Davis? Come, now—it's not
so difficult. By the way, you've been, if I may say so,
extraordinarily foolish. You've left me hunting about
for the third victim. As a result, you've been in serious
danger."

"Me? I don't know what you mean."

"I mean that you haven't been honest with me, Mrs. Davis. You held out on me—just as Mrs. Boyle held out on me."

"I don't understand."

"Oh, yes, you do. Why, when I first mentioned the Longridge Farm case, *you knew all about it.* Oh, yes, you did. You were upset. And it was you who confirmed that Mrs. Boyle was the billeting officer for this part of the country. Both you and she came from these parts. So when I began to speculate who the third victim was likely to be, I plumped at once for you. You'd shown firsthand knowledge of the Longridge Farm business. We policemen aren't so dumb as we look, you know."

Molly said in a low voice, "You don't understand. I didn't want to remember."

"I can understand that." His voice changed a little. "Your maiden name was Wainwright, wasn't it?"

"Yes."

"And you're just a little older than you pretend to be. In 1940, when this thing happened, you were the schoolteacher at Abbeyvale school."

"No!"

"Oh, yes, you were, Mrs. Davis."

"I wasn't, I tell you."

"The child who died managed to get a letter posted to you. He stole a stamp. The letter begged for help—help from his kind teacher. It's a teacher's business to find out why a child doesn't come to school. You didn't find out. You ignored the poor little devil's letter."

"Stop." Molly's cheeks were flaming. "It's my sister you are talking about. She was the schoolmistress. And she didn't ignore his letter. She was ill—with pneumonia. She never saw the letter until after the child was dead. It upset her dreadfully—dreadfully—she was a terribly sensitive person. But it wasn't her fault. It's because she took it to heart so dreadfully that I've never been able to bear being reminded of it. It's been a nightmare to me, always."

Molly's hands went to her eyes, covering them. When she took them away, Trotter was staring at her.

He said softly, "So it was your sister. Well, after all—" He gave a sudden queer smile. "It doesn't much matter, does it? Your sister—*my* brother—" He took something out of his pocket. He was smiling now, happily.

Molly stared at the object he held. "I always thought the police didn't carry revolvers," she said.

"*The police don't,*" said the young man. He went on, "But you see, Mrs. Davis, *I'm not a policeman*. I'm Jim. I'm Georgie's brother. You thought I was a policeman because I rang up from the call box in the village and said that Sergeant Trotter was on his way. Then I cut the telephone wires outside the house when I got here, so that you shouldn't be able to ring back to the police station."

Molly stared at him. The revolver was pointing at her now.

"Don't move, Mrs. Davis—and don't scream—or I pull the trigger at once."

He was still smiling. It was, Molly realized with horror, a child's smile. And his voice, when he spoke, was becoming a child's voice.

"Yes," he said, "I'm Georgie's brother. Georgie died at Longridge Farm. That nasty woman sent us there, and the farmer's wife was cruel to us, and you wouldn't help us—three little blind mice. I said then I'd kill you all when I grew up. I meant it. I've thought of it ever since." He frowned suddenly. "They bothered me a lot in the army—that doctor kept asking me questions— I had to get away. I was afraid they'd stop me doing what I wanted to do. But I'm grown up now. Grown-ups can do what they like."

Molly pulled herself together. *Talk to him,* she said to herself. *Distract his mind.*

"But, Jim, listen," she said. "You'll never get safely away."

His face clouded over. "Somebody's hidden my skis. I can't find them." He laughed. "But I daresay it will be all right. It's your husband's revolver. I took it out of his drawer. I daresay they'll think *he* shot you. Anyway— I don't much care. It's been such fun—all of it. Pretending! That woman in London, her face when she recognized me. That stupid woman this morning!"

He nodded his head.

Clearly, with eerie effect, came a whistle. Someone whistling the tune of "Three Blind Mice."

Trotter started, the revolver wavered—a voice shouted, "Down, Mrs. Davis."

Molly dropped to the floor as Major Metcalf, rising from behind the concealment of the sofa by the door flung himself upon Trotter. The revolver went off—and the bullet lodged in one of the somewhat mediocre oil paintings dear to the heart of the late Miss Emory.

A moment later, all was pandemonium—Giles rushed in, followed by Christopher and Mr. Paravicini.

Major Metcalf, retaining his grasp of Trotter, spoke in short explosive sentences.

"Came in while you were playing—slipped behind the sofa— I've been on to him from the beginning—that's to say, I knew he wasn't a police officer. *I'm* a police officer —Inspector Tanner. We arranged with Metcalf I should take his place. Scotland Yard thought it advisable to have someone on the spot. Now, my lad—" He spoke quite gently to the now docile Trotter. "You come with me. No one will hurt you. You'll be all right. We'll look after you."

In a piteous child's voice the bronzed young man asked, "Georgie won't be angry with me?"

Metcalf said, "No. Georgie won't be angry."

He murmured to Giles as he passed him, "Mad as a hatter, poor devil."

They went out together. Mr. Paravicini touched Christopher Wren on the arm.

"You, also, my friend," he said, "come with me."

Giles and Molly, left alone, looked at each other. In another moment they were in each other's arms.

"Darling," said Giles, "you're sure he didn't hurt you?"

"No, no, I'm quite all right. Giles, I've been so terribly mixed up. I almost thought you—why did you go to London that day?"

"Darling, I wanted to get you an anniversary present, for tomorrow. I didn't want you to know."

"How extraordinary! *I* went to London to get *you* a present and I didn't want you to know."

"I was insanely jealous of that neurotic ass. I must have been mad. Forgive me, darling."

The door opened, and Mr. Paravicini skipped in in his goatlike way. He was beaming.

"Interrupting the reconciliation— Such a charming scene— But, alas, I must bid you adieu. A police jeep has managed to get through. I shall persuade them to take me with them." He bent and whispered mysteriously in Molly's ear, "I may have a few embarrassments in the near future—but I am confident I can arrange matters, and if you should receive a case—with a goose, say, a turkey, some tins of *foie gras*, a ham—some nylon stockings, yes? Well, you understand, it will be with my compliments to a very charming lady. Mr. Davis, my check is on the hall table."

He kissed Molly's hand and skipped to the door.

"Nylons?" murmured Molly. "*Foie gras?* Who is Mr. Paravicini? Santa Claus?"

"Black-market style, I suspect," said Giles.

Christopher Wren poked a diffident head in. "My dears," he said, "I hope I'm not intruding, but there's a terrible smell of burning from the kitchen. Ought I to *do* something about it?"

With an anguished cry of *"My pie!"* Molly fled from the room.

Strange Jest

"AND THIS," SAID JANE HELIER, completing her introductions, "is Miss Marple!"

Being an actress, she was able to make her point. It was clearly the climax, the triumphant finale! Her tone was equally compounded of reverent awe and triumph.

The odd part of it was that the object thus proudly proclaimed was merely a gentle, fussy-looking, elderly spinster. In the eyes of the two young people who had just, by Jane's good offices, made her acquaintance, there showed incredulity and a tinge of dismay. They were nice-looking people; the girl, Charmian Stroud, slim and dark—the man, Edward Rossiter, a fair-haired, amiable young giant.

Charmian said a little breathlessly, "Oh! We're awfully pleased to meet you." But there was doubt in her eyes. She flung a quick, questioning glance at Jane Helier.

"Darling," said Jane, answering the glance, "she's absolutely *marvelous*. Leave it all to her. I told you I'd get her here and I have." She added to Miss Marple, *"You'll* fix it for them, I know. It will be easy for *you*."

Miss Marple turned her placid, china-blue eyes toward Mr. Rossiter. "Won't you tell me," she said, "what all this is about?"

"Jane's a friend of ours," Charmian broke in impatiently. "Edward and I are in rather a fix. Jane said if we would come to her party, she'd introduce us to someone who was—who would—who could—"

Edward came to the rescue. "Jane tells us you're the last word in sleuths, Miss Marple!"

The old lady's eyes twinkled, but she protested modestly. "Oh, no, no! Nothing of the kind. It's just that living in a village as I do, one gets to know so much about human nature. But really you have made me quite curious. Do tell me your problem."

"I'm afraid it's terribly hackneyed—just buried treasure," said Edward.

"Indeed? But that sounds most exciting!"

"I know. Like *Treasure Island*. But our problem lacks the usual romantic touches. No point on a chart indicated by a skull and crossbones, no directions like 'four paces to the left, west by north.' It's horribly prosaic—just where we ought to dig."

"Have you tried at all?"

"I should say we'd dug about two solid square acres! The whole place is ready to be turned into a market garden. We're just discussing whether to grow vegetable marrows or potatoes."

Charmian said rather abruptly, "May we really tell you all about it?"

"But, of course, my dear."

"Then let's find a peaceful spot. Come on, Edward." She led the way out of the overcrowded and smoke-laden room, and they went up the stairs, to a small sitting-room on the second floor.

When they were seated, Charmian began abruptly. "Well, here goes! The story starts with Uncle Mathew, uncle—or rather, great great-uncle—to both of us. He was incredibly ancient. Edward and I were his only relations. He was fond of us and always declared that when he died he would leave his money between us. Well, he died last March and left everything he had to be divided equally between Edward and myself. What I've just said sounds rather callous—I don't mean that it was right that he died—actually we were very fond of him. But he'd been ill for some time.

"The point is that the 'everything' he left turned out to be practically nothing at all. And that, frankly, was a bit of a blow to us both, wasn't it, Edward?"

The amiable Edward agreed. "You see," he said, "we'd counted on it a bit. I mean, when you know a good bit of money is coming to you, you don't—well—buckle down and try to make it yourself. I'm in the army—not got anything to speak of outside my pay—and Charmian herself hasn't got a bean. She works as a stage manager in a repertory theater—quite interesting, and she enjoys it—but no money in it. We'd counted on getting married, but weren't worried about the money side of it because we both knew we'd be jolly well off some day."

"And now, you see, we're not!" said Charmian. "What's more, Ansteys—that's the family place, and Edward and I both love it—will probably have to be sold. And Edward and I feel we just can't bear that! But if we don't find Uncle Mathew's money, we shall have to sell."

Edward said, "You know, Charmian, we still haven't come to the vital point."

"Well, you talk, then."

Edward turned to Miss Marple. "It's like this, you see. As Uncle Mathew grew older, he got more and more suspicious. He didn't trust anybody."

"Very wise of him," said Miss Marple. "The depravity of human nature is unbelievable."

"Well, you may be right. Anyway, Uncle Mathew thought so. He had a friend who lost his money in a bank, and another friend who was ruined by an absconding solicitor, and he lost some money himself in a fraudulent company. He got so that he used to hold forth at great length that the only safe and sane thing to do was to convert your money into solid bullion and bury it."

"Ah," said Miss Marple. "I begin to see."

"Yes. Friends argued with him, pointed out that he'd get no interest that way, but he held that that didn't really matter. The bulk of your money, he said, should be 'kept in a box under the bed or buried in the garden.' Those were his words."

Charmian went on. "And when he died, he left hardly anything at all in securities, though he was very rich. So we think that that's what he must have done."

Edward explained. "We found that he had sold securities and drawn out large sums of money from time to time, and nobody knows what he did with them. But it seems probable that he lived up to his principles, and that he did buy gold and bury it."

"He didn't say anything before he died? Leave any paper? No letter?"

"That's the maddening part of it. He didn't. He'd been unconscious for some days, but he rallied before he died. He looked at us both and chuckled—a faint, weak little chuckle. He said, *'You'll* be all right, my pretty pair of doves.' And then he tapped his eye—his right eye—and winked at us. And then—he died. Poor old Uncle Mathew."

"He tapped his eye," said Miss Marple thoughtfully.

Edward said eagerly, "Does that convey anything to you? It made me think of an Arsene Lupin story where there was something hidden in a man's glass eye. But Uncle Mathew didn't have a glass eye."

Miss Marple shook her head. "No—I can't think of anything at the moment."

Charmian said disappointedly, "Jane told us you'd say *at once* where to dig!"

Miss Marple smiled. "I'm not quite a conjurer, you know. I didn't know your uncle, or what sort of man he was, and I don't know the house or the grounds."

Charmian said, "If you did know them?"

"Well, it must be quite simple really, mustn't it?" said Miss Marple.

"Simple!" said Charmian. "You come down to Ansteys and see if it's simple!"

It is possible that she did not mean the invitation to be taken seriously, but Miss Marple said briskly, "Well, really, my dear, that's very kind of you. I've always wanted to have the chance of looking for buried treasure. And," she added, looking at them with a beaming, late-Victorian smile, "with a love interest, too!"

"You see!" said Charmian, gesturing dramatically.

They had just completed a grand tour of Ansteys. They had been round the kitchen garden—heavily trenched. They had been through the little woods, where every important tree had been dug round, and had gazed sadly on the pitted surface of the once smooth lawn. They had been up to the attic, where old trunks and chests had been rifled of their contents. They had been down to the cellars, where flagstones had been heaved unwillingly from their sockets. They had measured and tapped walls, and Miss Marple had been shown every antique piece of furniture that contained or could be suspected of containing a secret drawer.

On a table in the morning room there was a heap of papers—all the papers that the late Mathew Stroud had left. Not one had been destroyed, and Charmian and Edward were wont to return to them again and again, earnestly perusing bills, invitations, and business correspondence in the hope of spotting a hitherto unnoticed clue.

"Can you think of anywhere we haven't looked?" demanded Charmian hopefully.

Miss Marple shook her head. "You seem to have been very thorough, my dear. Perhaps, if I may say so, just a little *too* thorough. I always think, you know, that one should have a plan. It's like my friend, Mrs. Eldritch; she had such a nice little maid, polished linoleum beautifully, but she was so thorough that she polished the bathroom floor too much, and as Mrs. Eldritch was stepping out of the bath the cork mat slipped from under her, and she had a very nasty fall and actually broke her leg! Most awkward, because the bathroom door was locked, of course, and the gardener had to get a ladder and come in through the window—terribly distressing to Mrs. Eldritch, who had always been a very modest woman."

Edward moved restlessly.

Miss Marple said quickly, "Please forgive me. So apt, I know, to fly off at a tangent. But one thing does remind one of another. And sometimes that is helpful. All I was trying to say was that perhaps if we tried to sharpen our wits and think of a likely place—"

Edward said crossly, "You think of one, Miss Marple. Charmian's brains and mine are now only beautiful blanks!"

"Dear, dear. Of course—most tiring for you. If you don't mind I'll just look through all this." She indicated the papers on the table. "That is, if there's nothing private—I don't want to appear to pry."

"Oh, that's all right. But I'm afraid you won't find anything."

She sat down by the table and methodically worked through the sheaf of documents. As she replaced each one, she sorted them automatically into tidy little heaps. When she had finished she sat staring in front of her for some minutes.

Edward asked, not without a touch of malice, "Well, Miss Marple?"

Miss Marple came to herself with a little start. "I beg

your pardon. Most helpful."

"You've found something relevant?"

"Oh, no, nothing like that, but I do believe I know what sort of man your Uncle Mathew was. Rather like my own Uncle Henry, I think. Fond of rather obvious jokes. A bachelor, evidently—I wonder why—perhaps an early disappointment? Methodical up to a point, but not very fond of being tied up—so few bachelors are!"

Behind Miss Marple's back, Charmian made a sign to Edward. It said, *She's ga-ga.*

Miss Marple was continuing happily to talk of her deceased Uncle Henry. "Very fond of puns, he was. And to some people, puns are most annoying. A mere play upon words may be very irritating. He was a suspicious man, too. Always was convinced the servants were robbing him. And sometimes, of course, they were, but not always. It grew upon him, poor man. Toward the end he suspected them of tampering with his food, and finally refused to eat anything but boiled eggs! Said nobody could tamper with the inside of a boiled egg. Dear Uncle Henry, he used to be such a merry soul at one time— very fond of his coffee after dinner. He always used to say, 'This coffee is very Moorish,' meaning, you know, that he'd like a little more."

Edward felt that if he heard any more about Uncle Henry he'd go mad.

"Fond of young people, too," went on Miss Marple, "but inclined to tease them a little, if you know what I mean. Used to put bags of sweets where a child just couldn't reach them."

Casting politeness aside, Charmian said, "I think he sounds horrible!"

"Oh, no, dear, just an old bachelor, you know, and not used to children. And he wasn't at all stupid, really. He used to keep a good deal of money in the house, and he had a safe put in. Made a great fuss about it—and how very secure it was. As a result of his talking so much, burglars broke in one night and actually cut a hole in the safe with a chemical device."

"Served him right," said Edward.

"Oh, but there was nothing in the safe," said Miss Marple. "You see, he really kept the money somewhere else—behind some volumes of sermons in the library, as a matter of fact. He said people never took a book of that kind out of the shelf!"

Edward interrupted excitedly. "I say, that's an idea. What about the library?"

But Charmian shook a scornful head. "Do you think I hadn't thought of that? I went through all the books Tuesday of last week, when you went off to Portsmouth. Took them all out, shook them. Nothing there."

Edward sighed. Then, rousing himself, he endeavored to rid himself tactfully of their disappointing guest. "It's been awfully good of you to come down as you have and try to help us. Sorry it's been all a washout. Feel we trespassed a lot on your time. However—I'll get the car out, and you'll be able to catch the three-thirty—"

"Oh," said Miss Marple, "but we've got to find the money, haven't we? You mustn't give up, Mr. Rossiter. 'If at first you don't succeed, try, try, try again.' "

"You mean you're going to go—on trying?"

"Strickly speaking," said Miss Marple, "I haven't begun yet. 'First catch your hare—' as Mrs. Beeton says in her cookery book—a wonderful book but terribly expensive; most of the recipes begin, 'Take a quart of cream and a dozen eggs.' Let me see, where was I? Oh, yes. Well, we have, so to speak, caught our hare—the hare being, of course, your Uncle Mathew, and we've only got to decide now where he would have hidden the money. It ought to be quite simple."

"Simple?" demanded Charmian.

"Oh, yes, dear. I'm sure he would have done the obvious thing. A secret drawer—that's my solution."

Edward said dryly, "You couldn't put bars of gold in a secret drawer."

"No, no, of course not. But there's no reason to believe the money is in gold."

"He always used to say—"

"So did my Uncle Henry about his safe! So I should strongly suspect that that was just a simple blind. Diamonds—now they could be in a secret drawer quite easily."

"But we've looked in all the secret drawers. We had a cabinetmaker over to examine the furniture."

"Did you, dear? That was clever of you. I should suggest your uncle's own desk would be the most likely. Was it the tall escritoire against the wall there?"

"Yes. And I'll show you." Charmian went over to it. She took down the flap. Inside were pigeonholes and little drawers. She opened a small door in the center and touched a spring inside the left-hand drawer. The bottom of the center recess clicked and slid forward. Charmian drew it out, revealing a shallow well beneath. It was empty.

"Now isn't that a coincidence?" exclaimed Miss Marple. "Uncle Henry had a desk just like this, only his was burr walnut and this is mahogany."

"At any rate," said Charmian, "there's nothing there, as you can see."

"I expect," said Miss Marple, "your cabinetmaker was a young man. He didn't know everything. People were very artful when they made hiding-places in those days. There's such a thing as a secret inside a secret."

She extracted a hairpin from her neat bun of gray hair. Straightening it out, she stuck the point into what appeared to be a tiny wormhole in one side of the secret recess. With a little difficulty she pulled out a small drawer. In it was a bundle of faded letters and a folded paper.

Edward and Charmian pounced on the find together. With trembling fingers Edward unfolded the paper. He dropped it with an exclamation of disgust.

"A damned cookery recipe. Baked ham!"

Charmian was untying a ribbon that held the letters together. She drew one out and glanced at it. "Love letters!"

Miss Marple reacted with Victorian gusto. "How interesting! Perhaps the reason your uncle never married."

Charmian read aloud:

" 'My ever dear Mathew, I must confess that the time seems long indeed since I received your last letter. I try to occupy myself with the various tasks allotted to me, and often say to myself that I am indeed fortunate to see so much of the globe, though little did I think when I went to America that I should voyage off to these far islands!' "

Charmian broke off. "Where is it from? Oh! Hawaii!" She went on:

" 'Alas, these natives are still far from seeing the light. They are in an unclothed and savage state and spend most of their time swimming and dancing, adorning themselves with garlands of flowers. Mr. Gray has made some converts but it is uphill work, and he and Mrs. Gray get sadly discouraged. I try to do all I can to cheer and encourage him, but I, too, am often sad for a reason you can guess, dear Mathew. Alas, absence is a severe trial to a loving heart. Your renewed vows and protestations of affection cheered me greatly. Now and always you have my faithful and devoted heart, dear Mathew, and I remain— Your true love, Betty Martin.

" 'P.S.—I address my letter under cover to our mutual friend, Matilda Graves, as usual. I hope heaven will pardon this little subterfuge.' "

Edward whistled. "A female missionary! So that was Uncle Mathew's romance. I wonder why they never married?"

"She seems to have gone all over the world," said Charmian, looking through the letters. "Mauritius—all sorts of places. Probably died of yellow fever or something."

A gentle chuckle made them start. Miss Marple was apparently much amused. "Well, well," she said. "Fancy that, now!"

She was reading the recipe for baked ham. Seeing their inquiring glances, she read out: " 'Baked ham with spinach. Take a nice piece of gammon, stuff with cloves, and cover with brown sugar. Bake in a slow oven. Serve with a border of puréed spinach.' What do you think of that, now?"

"I think it sounds filthy," said Edward.

"No, no, actually it would be very good—but what do you think of *the whole thing?*"

A sudden ray of light illuminated Edward's face. "Do you think it's a code—cryptogram of some kind?" He seized it. "Look here, Charmian, it might be, you know! No reason to put a cooking-recipe in a secret drawer otherwise."

"Exactly," said Miss Marple. "Very, very significant."

Charmian said, "I know what it might be—invisible ink! Let's heat it. Turn on the electric fire."

Edward did so, but no signs of writing appeared under

the treatment.

Miss Marple coughed. "I really think, you know, that you're making it rather *too* difficult. The recipe is only an indication, so to speak. It is, I think, the letters that are significant."

"The letters?"

"Especially," said Miss Marple, "the signature."

But Edward hardly heard her. He called excitedly, "Charmian! Come here! She's right. See—the envelopes are old, right enough, but the letters themselves were written much later."

"Exactly," said Miss Marple.

"They're only fake old. I bet anything old Uncle Mat faked them himself—"

"Precisely," said Miss Marple.

"The whole thing's a sell. There never was a female missionary. It must be a code."

"My dear, dear children—there's really no need to make it all so difficult. Your uncle was really a very simple man. He had to have his little joke, that was all."

For the first time they gave her their full attention.

"Just exactly what do you mean, Miss Marple?" asked Charmian.

"I mean, dear, that you're actually holding the money in your hand this minute."

Charmian stared down.

"The signature, dear. That gives the whole thing away. The recipe is just an indication. Shorn of all the cloves and brown sugar and the rest of it, what is it *actually?* Why, gammon and spinach to be sure! *Gammon and spinach!* Meaning—nonsense! So it's clear that it's the letters that are important. And then, if you take into consideration what your uncle did just before he died. He tapped his eye, you said. Well, there you are—that gives you the clue, you see."

Charmian said, "Are we mad, or are you?"

"Surely, my dear, you must have heard the expression meaning that something is not a true picture, or has it quite died out nowadays? 'All my eye and Betty Martin'."

Edward gasped, his eyes falling to the letter in his hand. "Betty Martin—"

"Of course, Mr. Rossiter. As you have just said, there isn't—there wasn't any such person. The letters were written by your uncle, and I daresay he got a lot of fun out of writing them! As you say, the writing on the envelopes is much older—in fact, the envelopes couldn't belong to the letters, anyway, because the postmark of the one you are holding is 1851."

She paused. She made it very emphatic. "1851. And that explains everything, doesn't it?"

"Not to me," said Edward.

"Well, of course," said Miss Marple, "I daresay it wouldn't to me if it weren't for my great-nephew Lionel. Such a dear little boy and a passionate stamp collector. Knows all about stamps. It was he who told me about rare and expensive stamps and that a wonderful new find had come up for auction. And I actually remember his mentioning one stamp—an 1851 *blue two-cent*. It realized something like $25,000, I believe. Fancy! I should imagine that the other stamps are something also rare and expensive. No doubt your uncle bought through dealers and was careful to 'cover his tracks,' as they say in detective stories."

Edward groaned. He sat down and buried his face in his hands.

"What's the matter?" demanded Charmian.

"Nothing. It's only the awful thought that, but for Miss Marple, we might have burned these letters in a decent, gentlemanly way!"

"Ah," said Miss Marple, "that's just what these old

gentlemen who are fond of their joke never realize. My Uncle Henry, I remember, sent a favorite niece a five-pound note for a Christmas present. He put it inside a Christmas card, gummed the card together, and wrote on it, 'Love and best wishes. Afraid this is all I can manage this year.'

"She, poor girl, was annoyed at what she thought was his meanness and threw it all straight into the fire. So then, of course, he had to give her another."

Edward's feelings toward Uncle Henry had suffered an abrupt and complete change.

"Miss Marple," he said, "I'm going to get a bottle of champagne. We'll all drink the health of your Uncle Henry."

Tape-Measure Murder

MISS POLITT TOOK HOLD of the knocker and rapped politely on the cottage door. After a discreet interval she knocked again. The parcel under her left arm shifted a little as she did so, and she readjusted it. Inside the parcel was Mrs. Spenlow's new green winter dress, ready for fitting. From Miss Politt's left hand dangled a bag of black silk, containing a tape measure, a pincushion, and a large, practical pair of scissors.

Miss Politt was tall and gaunt, with a sharp nose, pursed lips, and meager iron-gray hair. She hesitated before using the knocker for the third time. Glancing down the street, she saw a figure rapidly approaching. Miss Hartnell, jolly, weather-beaten, fifty-five, shouted out in her usual loud bass voice, "Good afternoon, Miss Politt!"

The dressmaker answered, "Good afternoon, Miss Hartnell." Her voice was excessively thin and genteel in its accents. She had started life as a lady's maid. "Excuse me," she went on, "but do you happen to know if by any chance Mrs. Spenlow isn't at home?"

"Not the least idea," said Miss Hartnell.

"It's rather awkward, you see. I was to fit on Mrs. Spenlow's new dress this afternoon. Three-thirty, she said."

Miss Hartnell consulted her wrist watch. "It's a little past the half-hour now."

"Yes. I have knocked three times, but there doesn't seem to be any answer, so I was wondering if perhaps Mrs. Spenlow might have gone out and forgotten. She doesn't forget appointments as a rule, and she wants the dress to wear the day after tomorrow."

Miss Hartnell entered the gate and walked up the path to join Miss Politt outside the door of Laburnam Cottage.

"Why doesn't Gladys answer the door?" she demanded. "Oh, no, of course, it's Thursday—Gladys's day out. I expect Mrs. Spenlow has fallen asleep. I don't expect you've made enough noise with this thing."

Seizing the knocker, she executed a deafening *rat-a-tat-tat,* and in addition thumped upon the panels of the door. She also called out in a stentorian voice, "What ho, within there!"

There was no response.

Miss Politt murmured, "Oh, I think Mrs. Spenlow must have forgotten and gone out. I'll call round some other time." She began edging away down the path.

"Nonsense," said Miss Hartnell firmly. "She can't have gone out. I'd have met her. I'll just take a look through the windows and see if I can find any signs of life."

She laughed in her usual hearty manner, to indicate that it was a joke, and applied a perfunctory glance to the nearest windowpane—perfunctory because she knew quite well that the front room was seldom used, Mr. and Mrs. Spenlow preferring the small back sitting-room.

Perfunctory as it was, though, it succeeded in its object. Miss Hartnell, it is true, saw no signs of life. On the contrary, she saw, through the window, Mrs. Spenlow lying on the hearthrug—dead.

"Of course," said Miss Hartnell, telling the story afterward, "I managed to keep my head. That Politt creature wouldn't have had the least idea of what to do. 'Got to keep our heads,' I said to her. '*You* stay here, and I'll go for Constable Palk.' She said something about not wanting to be left, but I paid no attention at all. One has to be firm with that sort of person. I've always found they enjoy making a fuss. So I was just going off when,

to be artful."

Miss Marple said thoughtfully, "Mr. Spenlow?"

She liked Mr. Spenlow. He was a small, spare man, stiff and conventional in speech, the acme of respectability. It seemed odd that he should have come to live in the country, he had so clearly lived in towns all his life. To Miss Marple he confided the reason. He said, "I have always intended, ever since I was a small boy, to live in the country some day and have a garden of my own. I have always been very much attached to flowers. My wife, you know, kept a flower shop. That's where I saw her first."

A dry statement, but it opened up a vista of romance. A younger, prettier Mrs. Spenlow, seen against a background of flowers.

Mr. Spenlow, however, really knew nothing about flowers. He had no idea of seeds, of cuttings, of bedding out, of annuals or perennials. He had only a vision—a vision of a small cottage garden thickly planted with sweet-smelling, brightly colored blossoms. He had asked, almost pathetically, for instruction, and had noted down Miss Marple's replies to questions in a little book.

He was a man of quiet method. It was, perhaps, because of this trait, that the police were interested in him when his wife was found murdered. With patience and perseverance they learned a good deal about the late Mrs. Spenlow—and soon all St. Mary Mead knew it, too.

The late Mrs. Spenlow had begun life as a between-maid in a large house. She had left that position to marry the second gardener, and with him had started a flower shop in London. The shop had prospered. Not so the gardener, who before long had sickened and died.

His widow carried on the shop and enlarged it in an ambitious way. She had continued to prosper. Then she had sold the business at a handsome price and embarked upon matrimony for the second time—with Mr. Spenlow, a middle-aged jeweler who had inherited a small and struggling business. Not long afterward, they had sold the business and come down to St. Mary Mead.

Mrs. Spenlow was a well-to-do woman. The profits from her florist's establishment she had invested—"under spirit guidance," as she explained to all and sundry. The spirits had advised her with unexpected acumen.

All her investments had prospered, some in quite a sensational fashion. Instead, however, of this increasing her belief in spiritualism, Mrs. Spenlow basely deserted mediums and sittings, and made a brief but wholehearted plunge into an obscure religion with Indian affinities which was based on various forms of deep breathing. When, however, she arrived at St. Mary Mead, she had relapsed into a period of orthodox Church-of-England beliefs. She was a good deal at the vicarage, and attended church services with assiduity. She patronized the village shops, took an interest in the local happenings, and played village bridge.

A humdrum, everyday life. And—suddenly—murder.

Colonel Melchett, the chief constable, had summoned Inspector Slack.

Slack was a positive type of man. When he had made up his mind, he was sure. He was quite sure now. "Husband did it, sir," he said.

"You think so?"

"Quite sure of it. You've only got to look at him. Guilty as hell. Never showed a sign of grief or emotion. He came back to the house knowing she was dead."

"Wouldn't he at least have tried to act the part of the distracted husband?"

"Not him, sir. Too pleased with himself. Some gentlemen can't act. Too stiff."

"Any other woman in his life?" Colonel Melchett asked.

"Haven't been able to find any trace of one. Of course, he's the artful kind. He'd cover his tracks. As I see it, he was just fed up with his wife. She'd got the money, and I should say was a trying woman to live with—always taking up some 'ism' or other. He cold-bloodedly decided to do away with her and live comfortably on his own."

"Yes, that could be the case, I suppose."

"Depend upon it, that was it. Made his plans careful. Pretended to get a phone call—"

Melchett interrupted him. "No call been traced?"

"No, sir. That means either that he lied, or that the call was put through from a public telephone booth. The only two public phones in the village are at the station and the post office. Post office it certainly wasn't. Mrs. Blade sees everyone who comes in. Station it might be. Train arrives at two twenty-seven and there's a bit of a bustle then. But the main thing is *he* says it was Miss Marple who called him up, and that certainly isn't true. The call didn't come from her house, and she herself was away at the Institute."

"You're not overlooking the possibility that the husband was deliberately got out of the way—by someone who wanted to murder Mrs. Spenlow?"

"You're thinking of young Ted Gerard, aren't you, sir? I've been working on him—what we're up against there is lack of motive. He doesn't stand to gain anything."

"He's an undesirable character, though. Quite a pretty little spot of embezzlement to his credit."

"I'm not saying he isn't a wrong 'un. Still, he did go to his boss and own up to that embezzlement. And his employers weren't wise to it."

"An Oxford Grouper," said Melchett.

"Yes, sir. Became a convert and went off to do the straight thing and own up to having pinched money. I'm not saying, mind you, that it mayn't have been astuteness. He may have thought he was suspected and decided to gamble on honest repentance."

"You have a skeptical mind, Slack," said Colonel Melchett. "By the way, have you talked to Miss Marple at all?"

"What's *she* got to do with it, sir?"

"Oh, nothing. But she hears things, you know. Why don't you go and have a chat with her? She's a very sharp old lady."

Slack changed the subject. "One thing I've been meaning to ask you, sir. That domestic-service job where the deceased started her career—Sir Robert Abercrombie's place. That's where that jewel robbery was—emeralds—worth a packet. Never got them. I've been looking it up —must have happened when the Spenlow woman was there, though she'd have been quite a girl at the time. Don't think she was mixed up in it, do you, sir? Spenlow, you know, was one of those little tuppenny-ha'penny jewelers—just the chap for a fence."

Melchett shook his head. "Don't think there's anything in that. She didn't even know Spenlow at the time. I remember the case. Opinion in police circles was that a son of the house was mixed up in it—Jim Abercrombie —awful young waster. Had a pile of debts, and just after the robbery they were all paid off—some rich woman, so they said, but I don't know— Old Abercrombie hedged a bit about the case—tried to call the police off."

"It was just an idea, sir," said Slack.

Miss Marple received Inspector Slack with gratification, especially when she heard that he had been sent by

Colonel Melchett.

"Now, really, that is very kind of Colonel Melchett. I didn't know he remembered me."

"He remembers you, all right. Told me that what you didn't know of what goes on in St. Mary Mead isn't worth knowing."

"Too kind of him, but really I don't know anything at all. About this murder, I mean."

"You know what the talk about it is."

"Oh, of course—but it wouldn't do, would it, to repeat just idle talk?"

Slack said, with an attempt at geniality, "This isn't an official conversation, you know. It's in confidence, so to speak."

"You mean you really want to know what people are saying? Whether there's any truth in it or not?"

"That's the idea."

"Well, of course, there's been a great deal of talk and speculation. And there are really two distinct camps, if you understand me. To begin with, there are the people who think that the husband did it. A husband or a wife is, in a way, the natural person to suspect, don't you think so?"

"Maybe," said the inspector cautiously.

"Such close quarters, you know. Then, so often, the money angle. I hear that it was Mrs. Spenlow who had the money, and therefore Mr. Spenlow does benefit by her death. In this wicked world I'm afraid the most uncharitable assumptions are often justified."

"He comes into a tidy sum, all right."

"Just so. It would seem quite plausible, wouldn't it, for him to strangle her, leave the house by the back, come across the fields to my house, ask for me and pretend he'd had a telephone call from me, then go back and find his wife murdered in his absence—hoping, of course, that the crime would be put down to some tramp or burglar."

The inspector nodded. "What with the money angle —and if they'd been on bad terms lately—"

But Miss Marple interrupted him. "Oh, but they hadn't."

"You know that for a fact?"

"Everyone would have known if they'd quarreled! The maid, Gladys Brent—she'd have soon spread it round the village."

The inspector said feebly, "She mightn't have known—" and received a pitying smile in reply.

Miss Marple went on. "And then there's the other school of thought. Ted Gerard. A good-looking young man. I'm afraid, you know, that good looks are inclined to influence one more than they should. Our last curate but one—quite a magical effect! All the girls came to church—evening service as well as morning. And many older women became unusually active in parish work— and the slippers and scarfs that were made for him! Quite embarrassing for the poor young man.

"But let me see, where was I? Oh, yes, this young man, Ted Gerard. Of course, there has been talk about him. He's come down to see her so often. Though Mrs. Spenlow told me herself that he was a member of what I think they call the Oxford Group. A religious movement. They are quite sincere and very earnest, I believe, and Mrs. Spenlow was impressed by it all."

Miss Marple took a breath and went on. "And I'm sure there was no reason to believe that there was anything more in it than that, but you know what people are. Quite a lot of people are convinced that Mrs. Spenlow was infatuated with the young man, and that she'd lent him quite a lot of money. And it's perfectly true that he was actually seen at the station that day. In the train

—the two twenty-seven down train. But of course it would be quite easy, wouldn't it, to slip out of the other side of the train and go through the cutting and over the fence and round by the hedge and never come out of the station entrance at all. So that he need not have been seen going to the cottage. And, of course, people do think that what Mrs. Spenlow was wearing was rather peculiar."

"Peculiar?"

"A kimono. Not a dress." Miss Marple blushed. "That sort of thing, you know, is, perhaps, rather suggestive to some people."

"You think it was suggestive?"

"Oh, no, I don't think so. I think it was perfectly natural."

"You think it was natural?"

"Under the circumstances, yes." Miss Marple's glance was cool and reflective.

Inspector Slack said, "It might give us another motive for the husband. Jealousy."

"Oh, no, Mr. Spenlow would never be jealous. He's not the sort of man who notices things. If his wife had gone away and left a note on the pincushion, it would be the first he'd know of anything of that kind."

Inspector Slack was puzzled by the intent way she was looking at him. He had an idea that all her conversation was intended to hint at something he didn't understand. She said now, with some emphasis, "Didn't *you* find any clues, Inspector—on the spot?"

"People don't leave fingerprints and cigarette ash nowadays, Miss Marple."

"But this, I think," she suggested, "was an old-fashioned crime—"

Slack said sharply, "Now what do you mean by that?"

Miss Marple remarked slowly, "I think, you know, that

Constable Palk could help you. He was the first person on the—on the 'scene of the crime,' as they say."

Mr. Spenlow was sitting in a deck chair. He looked bewildered. He said, in his thin, precise voice, "I may, of course, be imagining what occurred. My hearing is not as good as it was. But I distinctly think I heard a small boy call after me, 'Yah, who's a Crippen?' It—it conveyed the impression to me that he was of the opinion that I had—had killed my dear wife."

Miss Marple, gently snipping off a dead rose head, said, "That was the impression he meant to convey, no doubt."

"But what could possibly have put such an idea into a child's head?"

Miss Marple coughed. "Listening, no doubt, to the opinions of his elders."

"You—you really mean that other people think that, also?"

"Quite half the people in St. Mary Mead."

"But—my dear lady—what can possibly have given rise to such an idea? I was sincerely attached to my wife. She did not, alas, take to living in the country as much as I had hoped she would do, but perfect agreement on every subject is an impossible ideal. I assure you I feel her loss very keenly."

"Probably. But if you will excuse my saying so, you don't sound as though you do."

Mr. Spenlow drew his meager frame up to its full height. "My dear lady, many years ago I read of a certain Chinese philosopher who, when his dearly loved wife was taken from him, continued calmly to beat a gong in the street—a customary Chinese pastime, I presume— exactly as usual. The people of the city were much impressed by his fortitude."

"But," said Miss Marple, "the people of St. Mary Mead react rather differently. Chinese philosophy does not appeal to them."

"But you understand?"

Miss Marple nodded. "My Uncle Henry," she explained, "was a man of unusual self-control. His motto was 'Never display emotion.' He, too, was very fond of flowers."

"I was thinking," said Mr. Spenlow with something like eagerness, "that I might, perhaps, have a pergola on the west side of the cottage. Pink roses and, perhaps, wisteria. And there is a white starry flower, whose name for the moment escapes me—"

In the tone in which she spoke to her grandnephew, aged three, Miss Marple said, "I have a very nice catalogue here, with pictures. Perhaps you would like to look through it—I have to go up to the village."

Leaving Mr. Spenlow sitting happily in the garden with his catalogue, Miss Marple went up to her room, hastily rolled up a dress in a piece of brown paper, and, leaving the house, walked briskly up to the post office. Miss Politt, the dressmaker, lived in rooms over the post office.

But Miss Marple did not at once go through the door and up the stairs. It was just two-thirty, and, a minute late, the Much Benham bus drew up outside the post-office door. It was one of the events of the day in St. Mary Mead. The postmistress hurried out with parcels, parcels connected with the shop side of her business, for the post office also dealt in sweets, cheap books, and children's toys.

For some four minutes Miss Marple was alone in the post office.

Not till the postmistress returned to her post did Miss Marple go upstairs and explain to Miss Politt that she wanted her old gray crepe altered and made more fashionable if that were possible. Miss Politt promised to see what she could do.

The chief constable was rather astonished when Miss Marple's name was brought to him. She came in with many apologies. "So sorry—so very sorry to disturb you. You are so busy, I know, but then you have always been so very kind, Colonel Melchett, and I felt I would rather come to you instead of to Inspector Slack. For one thing, you know, I should hate Constable Palk to get into any trouble. Strictly speaking, I suppose he shouldn't have touched anything at all."

Colonel Melchett was slightly bewildered. He said, "Palk? That's the St. Mary Mead constable, isn't it? What has he been doing?"

"He picked up a pin, you know. It was in his tunic. And it occurred to me at the time that it was quite probable he had actually picked it up in Mrs. Spenlow's house."

"Quite, quite. But after all, you know, what's a pin? Matter of fact he did pick the pin up just by Mrs. Spenlow's body. Came and told Slack about it yesterday—you put him up to that, I gather? Oughtn't to have touched anything, of course, but as I said, what's a pin? It was only a common pin. Sort of thing any woman might use."

"Oh, no, Colonel Melchett, that's where you're wrong. To a man's eye, perhaps, it looked like an ordinary pin, but it wasn't. It was a special pin, a very thin pin, the kind you buy by the box, the kind used mostly by dressmakers."

Melchett stared at her, a faint light of comprehension breaking in on him. Miss Marple nodded her head several times, eagerly.

"Yes, of course. It seems to me so obvious. She was in

her kimono because she was going to try on her new dress, and she went into the front room, and Miss Politt just said something about measurements and put the tape measure round her neck—and then all she'd have to do was to cross it and pull—quite easy, so I've heard. And then, of course, she'd go outside and pull the door to and stand there knocking as though she'd just arrived. But the pin shows she'd *already been in the house.*"

"And it was Miss Politt who telephoned to Spenlow?"

"Yes. From the post office at two-thirty—just when the bus comes and the post office would be empty."

Colonel Melchett said, "But my dear Miss Marple, why? In heaven's name, why? You can't have a murder without a motive."

"Well, I think, you know, Colonel Melchett, from all I've heard, that the crime dates from a long time back. It reminds me, you know, of my two cousins, Antony and Gordon. Whatever Antony did always went right for him, and with poor Gordon it was just the other way about. Race horses went lame, and stocks went down, and property depreciated. As I see it, the two women were in it together."

"In what?"

"The robbery. Long ago. Very valuable emeralds, so I've heard. The lady's maid and the tweeny. Because one thing hasn't been explained—how, when the tweeny married the gardener, did they have enough money to set up a flower shop?

"The answer is, it was her share of the—the swag, I think is the right expression. Everything she did turned out well. Money made money. But the other one, the lady's maid, must have been unlucky. She came down to being just a village dressmaker. Then they met again. Quite all right at first, I expect, until Mr. Ted Gerard came on the scene.

"Mrs. Spenlow, you see, was already suffering from conscience, and was inclined to be emotionally religious. This young man no doubt urged her to 'face up' and to 'come clean' and I daresay she was strung up to do so. But Miss Politt didn't see it that way. All she saw was that she might go to prison for a robbery she had committed years ago. So she made up her mind to put a stop to it all. I'm afraid, you know, that she was always rather a wicked woman. I don't believe she'd have turned a hair if that nice, stupid Mr. Spenlow had been hanged."

Colonel Melchett said slowly, "We can—er—verify your theory—up to a point. The identity of the Politt woman with the lady's maid at the Abercrombies', but—"

Miss Marple reassured him. "It will be all quite easy. She's the kind of woman who will break down at once when she's taxed with the truth. And then, you see, I've got her tape measure. I—er—abstracted it yesterday when I was trying on. When she misses it and thinks the police have got it—well, she's quite an ignorant woman and she'll think it will prove the case against her in some way."

She smiled at him encouragingly. "You'll have no trouble, I can assure you." It was the tone in which his favorite aunt had once assured him that he could not fail to pass his entrance examination into Sandhurst.

And he had passed.

The Case of the Perfect Maid

"OH, IF YOU PLEASE, MADAM, could I speak to you a moment?"

It might be thought that this request was in the nature of an absurdity, since Edna, Miss Marple's little maid, was actually speaking to her mistress at the moment.

Recognizing the idiom, however, Miss Marple said promptly, "Certainly, Edna, come in and shut the door. What is it?"

Obediently shutting the door, Edna advanced into the room, pleated the corner of her apron between her fingers, and swallowed once or twice.

"Yes, Edna?" said Miss Marple encouragingly.

"Oh, please, ma'am, it's my cousin, Gladdie."

"Dear me," said Miss Marple, her mind leaping to the worst—and, alas, the most usual conclusion. "Not—not in trouble?"

Edna hastened to reassure her. "Oh, no, ma'am, nothing of that kind. Gladdie's not that kind of girl. It's just that she's upset. You see, she's lost her place."

"Dear me, I am sorry to hear that. She was at Old Hall, wasn't she, with the Miss—Misses—Skinner?"

"Yes, ma'am, that's right, ma'am. And Gladdie's very upset about it—very upset indeed."

"Gladys has changed places rather often before, though, hasn't she?"

"Oh, yes, ma'am. She's always one for a change, Gladdie is. She never seems to get really settled, if you know what I mean. But she's always been the one to give the notice, you see!"

"And this time it's the other way round?" asked Miss

Marple dryly.

"Yes, ma'am, and it's upset Gladdie something awful."

Miss Marple looked slightly surprised. Her recollection of Gladys, who had occasionally come to drink tea in the kitchen on her 'days out,' was a stout, giggling girl of unshakably equable temperament.

Edna went on. "You see, ma'am, it's the way it happened—the way Miss Skinner looked."

"How," inquired Miss Marple patiently, "did Miss Skinner look?"

This time Edna got well away with her news bulletin.

"Oh, ma'am, it was ever such a shock to Gladdie. You see, one of Miss Emily's brooches was missing, and such a hue and cry for it as never was, and of course nobody likes a thing like that to happen; it's upsetting, ma'am, if you know what I mean. And Gladdie's helped search everywhere, and there was Miss Lavinia saying she was going to the police about it, and then it turned up again, pushed right to the back of a drawer in the dressing-table, and very thankful Gladdie was.

"And the very next day as ever was a plate got broken, and Miss Lavinia she bounced out right away and told Gladdie to take a month's notice. And what Gladdie feels is it couldn't have been the plate and that Miss Lavinia was just making an excuse of that, and that it must be because of the brooch and they think as she took it and put it back when the police was mentioned, and Gladdie wouldn't do such a thing, not never she wouldn't, and what she feels is as it will get round and tell against her and it's a very serious thing for a girl, as you know, ma'am."

Miss Marple nodded. Though having no particular liking for the bouncing, self-opinioned Gladys, she was quite sure of the girl's intrinsic honesty and could well imagine that the affair must have upset her.

Edna said wistfully, "I suppose, ma'am, there isn't anything you could do about it? Gladdie's in ever such a taking."

"Tell her not to be silly," said Miss Marple crisply. "If she didn't take the brooch—which I'm sure she didn't —then she has no cause to be upset."

"It'll get about," said Edna dismally.

Miss Marple said, "I—er—am going up that way this afternoon. I'll have word with the Misses Skinner."

"Oh, thank you, madam," said Edna.

Old Hall was a big Victorian house surrounded by woods and park land. Since it had been proved unlettable and unsalable as it was, an enterprising speculator had divided it into four flats with a central hot-water system, and the use of 'the grounds' to be held in common by the tenants. The experiment had been satisfactory. A rich and eccentric old lady and her maid occupied one flat. The old lady had a passion for birds and entertained a feathered gathering to meals every day. A retired Indian judge and his wife rented a second. A very young couple, recently married, occupied the third, and the fourth had been taken only two months ago by two maiden ladies of the name of Skinner. The four sets of tenants were only on the most distant terms with each other, since none of them had anything in common. The landlord had been heard to say that this was an excellent thing. What he dreaded were friendships followed by estrangements and subsequent complaints to him.

Miss Marple was acquainted with all the tenants, though she knew none of them well. The elder Miss Skinner, Miss Lavinia, was what might be termed the working member of the firm. Miss Emily, the younger, spent most of her time in bed suffering from various complaints which, in the opinion of St. Mary Mead, were largely imaginary. Only Miss Lavinia believed devoutly in her sister's martyrdom and patience under affliction, and willingly ran errands and trotted up and down to the village for things that "my sister had suddenly fancied."

It was the view of St. Mary Mead that if Miss Emily suffered half as much as she said she did, she would have sent for Doctor Haydock long ago. But Miss Emily, when this was hinted to her, shut her eyes in a superior way and murmured that her case was not a simple one—the best specialists in London had been baffled by it—and that a wonderful new man had put her on a most revolutionary course of treatment and that she really hoped her health would improve under it. No humdrum G.P. could possibly understand her case.

"And it's my opinion," said the outspoken Miss Hartnell, "that she's very wise not to send for him. Dear Doctor Haydock, in that breezy manner of his, would tell her that there was nothing the matter with her and to get up and not make a fuss! Do her a lot of good!"

Failing such arbitrary treatment, however, Miss Emily continued to lie on sofas, to surround herself with strange little pill boxes, and to reject nearly everything that had been cooked for her and ask for something else—usually something difficult and inconvenient to get.

The door was opened to Miss Marple by "Gladdie," looking more depressed than Miss Marple had ever thought possible. In the sitting-room (a quarter of the late drawing-room, which had been partitioned into a dining-room, drawing-room, bathroom, and housemaid's cupboard), Miss Lavinia rose to greet Miss Marple.

Lavinia Skinner was a tall, gaunt, bony female of fifty. She had a gruff voice and an abrupt manner.

"Nice to see you," she said. "Emily's lying down—feeling low today, poor dear. Hope she'll see you, it would cheer her up, but there are times when she doesn't feel up to seeing anybody. Poor dear, she's wonderfully patient."

Miss Marple responded politely. Servants were the main topic of conversation in St. Mary Mead, so it was not difficult to lead the conversation in that direction. Miss Marple said she had heard that that nice girl, Gladys Holmes, was leaving.

Miss Lavinia nodded. "Wednesday week. Broke things, you know. Can't have that."

Miss Marple sighed and said we all had to put up with things nowadays. It was so difficult to get girls to come to the country. Did Miss Skinner really think it was wise to part with Gladys?

"Know it's difficult to get servants," admitted Miss Lavinia. "The Devereuxs haven't got anybody—but then, I don't wonder—always quarreling, jazz on all night—meals any time—that girl knows nothing of housekeeping, I pity her husband! Then the Larkins have just lost their maid. Of course, what with the judge's Indian temper and his wanting chota hazri, as he calls it, at six in the morning and Mrs. Larkin always fussing, I don't wonder at that, either. Mrs. Carmichael's Janet is a fixture, of course—though in my opinion she's the most disagreeable woman, and absolutely bullies the old lady."

"Then don't you think you might reconsider your decision about Gladys? She really is a nice girl. I know all her family; very honest and superior."

Miss Lavinia shook her head.

"I've got my reasons," she said importantly.

Miss Marple murmured, "You missed a brooch, I understand—"

"Now, who has been talking? I suppose the girl has.

Quite frankly, I'm almost certain she took it. And then got frightened and put it back—but, of course, one can't say anything unless one is sure." She changed the subject. "Do come and see Miss Emily, Miss Marple. I'm sure it would do her good."

Miss Marple followed meekly to where Miss Lavinia knocked on a door, was bidden enter, and ushered her guest into the best room in the flat, most of the light of which was excluded by half-drawn blinds. Miss Emily was lying in bed, apparently enjoying the half-gloom and her own indefinite sufferings.

The dim light showed her to be a thin, indecisive-looking creature, with a good deal of grayish-yellow hair untidily wound around her head and erupting into curls, the whole thing looking like a bird's nest of which no self-respecting bird could be proud. There was a smell in the room of Eau de Cologne, stale biscuits, and camphor.

With half-closed eyes and in a thin, weak voice, Emily Skinner explained that this was "one of her bad days."

"The worst of ill health is," said Miss Emily in a melancholy tone, "that one knows what a burden one is to everyone around one.

"Lavinia is very good to me. Lavvie dear, I do so hate giving trouble but if my hot-water bottle could only be filled in the way I like it—too full it weighs on me so—on the other hand, if it is not sufficiently filled, it gets cold immediately!"

"I'm sorry, dear. Give it to me. I will empty a little out."

"Perhaps, if you're doing that, it might be refilled. There are no rusks in the house, I suppose—no, no, it doesn't matter. I can do without. Some weak tea and a slice of lemon—no lemons? No, really, I couldn't drink tea without lemon. I think the milk was slightly turned this morning. It has put me right against milk in my tea. It doesn't matter. I can do without my tea. Only I do feel so weak. Oysters, they say, are nourishing. I wonder if I could fancy a few? No, no, too much bother to get hold of them so late in the day. I can fast until tomorrow."

Lavinia left the room murmuring something incoherent about bicycling down to the village.

Miss Emily smiled feebly at her guest and remarked that she did hate giving anyone any trouble.

Miss Marple told Edna that evening that she was afraid her embassy had met with no success.

She was rather troubled to find that rumors as to Gladys's dishonesty were already going around the village.

In the post office, Miss Wetherby tackled her. "My dear Jane, they gave her a written reference saying she was willing and sober and respectable, but saying nothing about honesty. That seems to me most significant! I hear there was some trouble about a brooch. I think there must be something in it, you know, because one doesn't let a servant go nowadays unless it's something rather grave. They'll find it most difficult to get anyone else. Girls simply will not go to Old Hall. They're nervous coming home on their days out. You'll see, the Skinners won't find anyone else, and then, perhaps that dreadful hypochondriac sister will have to get up and do something!"

Great was the chagrin of the village when it was made known that the Misses Skinner had engaged, from an agency, a new maid who, by all accounts, was a perfect paragon.

"A three years' reference recommending her most warmly, she prefers the country, and actually asks less wages than Gladys. I really feel we have been most fortunate."

"Well, really," said Miss Marple, to whom these details were imparted by Miss Lavinia in the fishmonger's shop. "It does seem too good to be true."

It then became the opinion of St. Mary Mead that the paragon would cry off at the last minute and fail to arrive.

None of these prognostications came true, however, and the village was able to observe the domestic treasure, by name, Mary Higgins, driving through the village in Reed's taxi to Old Hall. It had to be admitted that her appearance was good. A most respectable-looking woman, very neatly dressed.

When Miss Marple next visited Old Hall, on the occasion of recruiting stall-holders for the vicarage fete, Mary Higgins opened the door. She was certainly a most superior-looking maid, at a guess forty years of age, with neat black hair, rosy cheeks, a plump figure discreetly arrayed in black with a white apron and cap—"quite the good, old-fashioned type of servant," as Miss Marple explained afterward, and with the proper, inaudible, respectful voice, so different from the loud but adenoidal accents of Gladys.

Miss Lavinia was looking far less harassed than usual and, although she regretted that she could not take a stall owing to her preoccupation with her sister, she nevertheless tendered a handsome monetary contribution, and promised to produce a consignment of pen-wipers and babies' socks.

Miss Marple commented on her air of well-being.

"I really feel I owe a great deal to Mary. I am so thankful I had the resolution to get rid of that other girl. Mary is really invaluable. Cooks nicely and waits beautifully and keeps our little flat scrupulously clean—mattresses turned over every day. And she is really wonderful with Emily!"

Miss Marple hastily inquired after Emily.

"Oh, poor dear, she has been very much under the weather lately. She can't help it, of course, but it really makes things a little difficult sometimes. Wanting certain things cooked and then, when they come, saying she can't eat now—and then wanting them again half an hour later and everything spoiled and having to be done again. It makes, of course, a lot of work—but fortunately Mary does not seem to mind at all. She's used to waiting on invalids, she says, and understands them. It is such a comfort."

"Dear me," said Miss Marple. "You are fortunate."

"Yes, indeed. I really feel Mary has been sent to us as an answer to prayer."

"She sounds to me," said Miss Marple, "almost too good to be true. I should—well, I should be a little careful if I were you."

Lavinia Skinner failed to perceive the point of this remark. She said, "Oh! I assure you I do all I can to make her comfortable. I don't know what I should do if she left."

"I don't expect she'll leave until she's ready to leave," said Miss Marple and stared very hard at her hostess.

Miss Lavinia said, "If one has no domestic worries, it takes such a load off one's mind, doesn't it? How is your little Edna shaping?"

"She's doing quite nicely. Not much ahead, of course. Not like your Mary. Still I do know all about Edna because she's a village girl."

As she went out into the hall she heard the invalid's voice fretfully raised. "This compress has been allowed to get quite dry—Doctor Allerton particularly said moisture continually renewed. There, there, leave it. I want a cup of tea and a boiled egg—boiled only three minutes and a half, remember, and send Miss Lavinia to me."

The efficient Mary emerged from the bedroom and, saying to Lavinia, "Miss Emily is asking for you, madam," proceeded to open the door for Miss Marple, helping her into her coat and handing her her umbrella in the most irreproachable fashion.

Miss Marple took the umbrella, dropped it, tried to pick it up, and dropped her bag, which flew open. Mary politely retrieved various odds and ends—a handkerchief, an engagement book, an old-fashioned leather purse, two shillings, three pennies, and a striped piece of peppermint rock.

Miss Marple received the last with some signs of confusion.

"Oh, dear, that must have been Mrs. Clement's little boy. He was sucking it, I remember, and he took my bag to play with. He must have put it inside. It's terribly sticky, isn't it?"

"Shall I take it, madam?"

"Oh, would you? Thank you so much."

Mary stooped to retrieve the last item, a small mirror upon recovering which Miss Marple exclaimed fervently, "How lucky, now, that that isn't broken."

She thereupon departed, Mary standing politely by the door holding a piece of striped rock with a completely expressionless face.

For ten days longer St. Mary Mead had to endure hearing of the excellencies of Miss Lavinia's and Miss Emily's treasure.

On the eleventh day, the village awoke to its big thrill.

Mary, the paragon, was missing! Her bed had not been slept in, and the front door was found ajar. She had slipped out quietly during the night.

And not Mary alone was missing! Two brooches and five rings of Miss Lavinia's; three rings, a pendant, a bracelet, and four brooches of Miss Emily's were missing, also!

It was the beginning of a chapter of catastrophe.

Young Mrs. Devereux had lost her diamonds which she kept in an unlocked drawer and also some valuable furs given to her as a wedding present. The judge and his wife also had had jewelry taken and a certain amount of money. Mrs. Carmichael was the greatest sufferer. Not only had she some very valuable jewels but she also kept in the flat a large sum of money which had gone. It had been Janet's evening out, and her mistress was in the habit of walking round the gardens at dusk calling to the birds and scattering crumbs. It seemed clear that Mary, the perfect maid, had had keys to fit all the flats!

There was, it must be confessed, a certain amount of ill-natured pleasure in St. Mary Mead. Miss Lavinia had boasted so much of her marvelous Mary.

"And all the time, my dear, just a common thief!"

Interesting revelation followed. Not only had Mary disappeared into the blue, but the agency who had provided her and vouched for her credentials was alarmed to find that the Mary Higgins who had applied to them and whose references they had taken up had, to all intents and purposes, never existed. It was the name of a bona fide servant who had lived with the bona fide sister of a dean, but the real Mary Higgins was existing peacefully in a place in Cornwall.

"Damned clever, the whole thing," Inspector Slack was forced to admit. "And, if you ask me, that woman works in with a gang. There was a case of much the same kind in Northumberland a year ago. Stuff was never traced, and they never caught her. However, we'll do better than that in Much Benham!"

Inspector Slack was always a confident man.

Nevertheless, weeks passed, and Mary Higgins remained triumphantly at large. In vain Inspector Slack redoubled that energy that so belied his name.

Miss Lavinia remained tearful. Miss Emily was so upset, and felt so alarmed by her condition that she actually sent for Doctor Haydock.

The whole of the village was terribly anxious to know what he thought of Miss Emily's claims to ill health, but naturally could not ask him. Satisfactory data came to hand on the subject, however, through Mr. Meek, the chemist's assistant, who was walking out with Clara, Mrs. Price-Ridley's maid. It was then known that Doctor Haydock had prescribed a mixture of asafetida and valerian which, according to Mr. Meek, was the stock remedy for malingerers in the army!

Soon afterward it was learned that Miss Emily, not relishing the medical attention she had had, was declaring that in the state of her health she felt it her duty to be near the specialist in London who understood her case. It was, she said, only fair to Lavinia.

The flat was put up for subletting.

It was a few days after that that Miss Marple, rather pink and flustered, called at the police station in Much Benham and asked for Inspector Slack.

Inspector Slack did not like Miss Marple. But he was aware that the chief constable, Colonel Melchett, did not share that opinion. Rather grudgingly, therefore, he received her.

"Good afternoon, Miss Marple, what can I do for you?"

"Oh, dear," said Miss Marple, "I'm afraid you're in a hurry."

"Lots of work on," said Inspector Slack, "but I can spare a few moments."

"Oh, dear," said Miss Marple. "I hope I shall be able to put what I say properly. So difficult, you know, to explain oneself, don't you think? No, perhaps you don't. But you see, not having been educated in the modern style—just a governess, you know, who taught one the dates of the kings of England and general knowledge— Doctor Brewer—three kinds of diseases of wheat—blight, mildew—now what was the third—was it smut?"

"Do you want to talk about smut?" asked Inspector Slack and then blushed.

"Oh, no, no." Miss Marple hastily disclaimed any wish to talk about smut. "Just an illustration, you know. And how needles are made, and all that. Discursive, you know, but not teaching one to keep to the point. Which is what I want to do. It's about Miss Skinner's maid, Gladys, you know."

"Mary Higgins," said Inspector Slack.

"Oh, yes, the second maid. But it's Gladys Holmes I mean—rather an impertinent girl and far too pleased with herself but really strictly honest, and it's so important that that should be recognized."

"No charge against her so far as I know," said the Inspector.

"No, I know there isn't a charge—but that makes it worse. Because, you see, people go on thinking things. Oh, dear—I knew I should explain badly. What I really mean is that the important thing is to find Mary Higgins."

"Certainly," said Inspector Slack. "Have you any ideas on the subject?"

"Well, as a matter of fact, I have," said Miss Marple. "May I ask you a question? Are fingerprints of no use to you?"

"Ah," said Inspector Slack, "that's where she was a bit too artful for us. Did most of her work in rubber gloves or housemaid's gloves, it seems. And she'd been careful —wiped off everything in her bedroom and on the sink.

Couldn't find a single fingerprint in the place!"

"If you did have her fingerprints, would it help?"

"It might, madam. They may be known at the Yard. This isn't her first job, I'd say!"

Miss Marple nodded brightly. She opened her bag and extracted a small cardboard box. Inside it, wedged in cotton wool, was a small mirror.

"From my handbag," said Miss Marple. "The maid's prints are on it. I think they should be satisfactory—she touched an extremely sticky substance a moment previously."

Inspector Slack stared. "Did you get her fingerprints on purpose?"

"Of course."

"You suspected her then?"

"Well, you know it did strike me that she was a little too good to be true. I practically told Miss Lavinia so. But she simply wouldn't take the hint! I'm afraid, you know, Inspector, that I don't believe in paragons. Most of us have our faults—and domestic service shows them up very quickly!"

"Well," said Inspector Slack, recovering his balance, "I'm obliged to you, I'm sure. We'll send these up to the Yard and see what they have to say."

He stopped. Miss Marple had put her head a little on one side and was regarding him with a good deal of meaning.

"You wouldn't consider, I suppose, Inspector, looking a little nearer home?"

"What do you mean, Miss Marple?"

"It's very difficult to explain, but when you come across a peculiar thing you notice it. Although, often, peculiar things may be the merest trifles. I've felt that all along, you know; I mean about Gladys and the brooch. She's an honest girl; she didn't take that brooch. Then why did Miss Skinner think she did? Miss Skinner's not a fool; far from it! Why was she so anxious to let a girl go who was a good servant when servants are hard to get? It was peculiar, you know. So I wondered. I wondered a good deal. And I noticed another peculiar thing! Miss Emily's a hypochondriac, but she's the first hypochondriac who hasn't sent for some doctor or other at once. Hypochondriacs love doctors. Miss Emily didn't!"

"What are you suggesting, Miss Marple?"

"Well, I'm suggesting, you know, that Miss Lavinia and Miss Emily are peculiar people. Miss Emily spends nearly all her time in a dark room. And if that hair of hers isn't a wig I—I'll eat my own back switch! And what I say is this—it's perfectly possible for a thin, pale, gray-haired, whining woman to be the same as a black-haired, rosy-cheeked, plump woman. And nobody that I can find ever saw Miss Emily and Mary Higgins at one and the same time.

"Plenty of time to get impressions of all the keys, plenty of time to find out all about the other tenants, and then—get rid of the local girl. Miss Emily takes a brisk walk across country one night and arrives at the station as Mary Higgins next day. And then, at the right moment, Mary Higgins disappears, and off goes .the hue and cry after her. I'll tell you where you'll find her, Inspector. On Miss Emily Skinner's sofa! Get her finger-prints if you don't believe me, but you'll find I'm right! A couple of clever thieves, that's what the Skinners are —and no doubt in league with a clever post and rails or fence or whatever you call it. But they won't get away with it this time! I'm not going to have one of our village girl's character for honesty taken away like that! Gladys Holmes is as honest as the day, and everybody's going to know it! Good afternoon!"

Miss Marple had stalked out before Inspector Slack

had recovered.

"Whew!" he muttered. "I wonder if she's right?"

He soon found out that Miss Marple was right again.

Colonel Melchett congratulated Slack on his efficiency, and Miss Marple had Gladys come to tea with Edna and spoke to her seriously on settling down in a good situation when she got one.

The Case of the Caretaker

"WELL," DEMANDED DOCTOR HAYDOCK of his patient. "And how goes it today?"

Miss Marple smiled at him wanly from pillows.

"I suppose, really, that I'm better," she admitted, "but I feel so terribly depressed. I can't help feeling how much better it would have been if I had died. After all, I'm an old woman. Nobody wants me or cares about me."

Doctor Haydock interrupted with his usual brusqueness. "Yes, yes, typical afterreaction to this type of flu. What you need is something to take you out of yourself. A mental tonic."

Miss Marple sighed and shook her head.

"And what's more," continued Doctor Haydock, "I've brought my medicine with me!"

He tossed a long envelope onto the bed.

"Just the thing for you. The kind of puzzle that is right up your street."

"A puzzle?" Miss Marple looked interested.

"Literary effort of mine," said the doctor, blushing a little. "Tried to make a regular story of it. 'He said,' 'she said,' 'the girl thought,' etc. Facts of the story are true."

"But why a puzzle?" asked Miss Marple.

Doctor Haydock grinned. "Because the interpretation is up to you. I want to see if you're as clever as you always make out."

With that Parthian shot he departed.

Miss Marple picked up the manuscript and began to read.

"And where is the bride?" asked Miss Harmon genially.

The village was all agog to see the rich and beautiful young wife that Harry Laxton had brought back from abroad. There was a general indulgent feeling that Harry—wicked young scapegrace—had had all the luck. Everyone had always felt indulgent toward Harry. Even the owners of windows that had suffered from his indiscriminate use of a catapult had found their indignation dissipated by young Harry's abject expression of regret. He had broken windows, robbed orchards, poached rabbits, and later had run into debt, got entangled with the local tobacconist's daughter—been disentangled and sent off to Africa—and the village as represented by various aging spinsters had murmured indulgently, "Ah, well! Wild oats! He'll settle down!"

And now, sure enough, the prodigal had returned—not in affliction, but in triumph. Harry Laxton had "made good" as the saying goes. He had pulled himself together, worked hard, and had finally met and successfully wooed a young Anglo-French girl who was the possessor of a considerable fortune.

Harry might have lived in London, or purchased an estate in some fashionable hunting county, but he preferred to come back to the part of the world that was home to him. And there, in the most romantic way, he purchased the derelict estate in the dower house of which he had passed his childhood.

Kingsdean House had been unoccupied for nearly seventy years. It had gradually fallen into decay and abandon. An elderly caretaker and his wife lived in the one habitable corner of it. It was a vast, unprepossessing, grandiose mansion, the gardens overgrown with rank vegetation and the trees hemming it in like some gloomy enchanter's den.

The dower house was a pleasant, unpretentious house and had been let for a long term of years to Major Laxton, Harry's father. As a boy, Harry had roamed over the Kingsdean estate and knew every inch of the tangled woods, and the old house itself had always fascinated him.

Major Laxton had died some years ago, so it might have been thought that Harry would have had no ties to bring him back—nevertheless it was to the home of his boyhood that Harry brought his bride. The ruined old Kingsdean House was pulled down. An army of builders and contractors swooped down upon the place, and in almost a miraculously short space of time—so marvelously does wealth tell—the new house rose white and gleaming among the trees.

Next came a posse of gardeners and after them a procession of furniture vans.

The house was ready. Servants arrived. Lastly, a costly limousine deposited Harry and Mrs. Harry at the front door.

The village rushed to call, and Mrs. Price, who owned the largest house, and who considered herself to lead society in the place, sent out cards of invitation for a party "to meet the bride."

It was a great event. Several ladies had new frocks for the occasion. Everyone was excited, curious, anxious to see this fabulous creature. They said it was all so like a fairy story!

Miss Harmon, weather-beaten, hearty spinster, threw out her question as she squeezed her way through the crowded drawing-room door. Little Miss Brent, a thin, acidulated spinster, fluttered out information.

"Oh, my dear, quite charming. Such pretty manners. And quite young. Really, you know, it makes one feel quite envious to see someone who has everything like that. Good looks and money and breeding—most distinguished, nothing in the least common about her—and dear Harry so devoted!"

"Ah," said Miss Harmon, "it's early days yet!"

Miss Brent's thin nose quivered appreciatively. "Oh, my dear, do you really think—"

"We all know what Harry is," said Miss Harmon.

"We know what he was! But I expect now—"

"Ah," said Miss Harmon, "men are always the same. Once a gay deceiver, always a gay deceiver. I know them."

"Dear, dear. Poor young thing." Miss Brent looked much happier. "Yes, I expect she'll have trouble with him. Someone ought really to warn her. I wonder if she's heard anything of the old story?"

"It seems so very unfair," said Miss Brent, "that she should know nothing. So awkward. Especially with only the one chemist's shop in the village."

For the erstwhile tobacconist's daughter was now married to Mr. Edge, the chemist.

"It would be so much nicer," said Miss Brent, "if Mrs. Laxton were to deal with Boots in Much Benham."

"I daresay," said Miss Harmon, "that Harry Laxton will suggest that himself."

And again a significant look passed between them.

"But I certainly think," said Miss Harmon, "that she ought to know."

"Beasts!" said Clarice Vane indignantly to her uncle, Doctor Haydock. "Absolute beasts some people are."

He looked at her curiously.

She was a tall, dark girl, handsome, warmhearted and impulsive. Her big brown eyes were alight now with indignation as she said, "All these cats—saying things—

hinting things."

"About Harry Laxton?"

"Yes, about his affair with the tobacconist's daughter."

"Oh, that!" The doctor shrugged his shoulders. "A great many young men have affairs of that kind."

"Of course they do. And it's all over. So why harp on it? And bring it up years after? It's like ghouls feasting on dead bodies."

"I daresay, my dear, it does seem like that to you. But you see, they have very little to talk about down here, and so I'm afraid they do tend to dwell upon past scandals. But I'm curious to know why it upsets you so much?"

Clarice Vane bit her lip and flushed. She said, in a curiously muffled voice, "They—they look so happy. The Laxtons, I mean. They're young and in love, and it's all so lovely for them. I hate to think of it being spoiled by whispers and hints and innuendoes and general beastliness."

"H'm. I see."

Clarice went on. "He was talking to me just now. He's so happy and eager and excited and—yes, thrilled—at having got his heart's desire and rebuilt Kingsdean. He's like a child about it all. And she—well, I don't suppose anything has ever gone wrong in her whole life. She's always had everything. You've seen her. What did you think of her?"

The doctor did not answer at once. For other people, Louise Laxton might be an object of envy. A spoiled darling of fortune. To him she had brought only the refrain of a popular song heard many years ago, *Poor little rich girl—*

A small, delicate figure, with flaxen hair curled rather stiffly round her face and big, wistful blue eyes.

Louise was drooping a little. The long stream of congratulations had tired her. She was hoping it might soon be time to go. Perhaps, even now, Harry might say so. She looked at him sideways. So tall and broad-shouldered with his eager pleasure in this horrible, dull party.

Poor little rich girl—

"Ooph!" It was a sigh of relief.

Harry turned to look at his wife amusedly. They were driving away from the party.

She said, "Darling, what a frightful party!"

Harry laughed. "Yes, pretty terrible. Never mind, my sweet. It had to be done, you know. All these old pussies knew me when I lived here as a boy. They'd have been terribly disappointed not to have got a good look at you close up."

Louise made a grimace. She said, "Shall we have to see a lot of them?"

"What? Oh, no. They'll come and make ceremonious calls with card cases, and you'll return the calls and then you needn't bother any more. You can have your own friends down or whatever you like."

Louise said, after a minute or two, "Isn't there anyone amusing living down here?"

"Oh, yes. There's the County, you know. Though you may find them a bit dull, too. Mostly interested in bulbs and dogs and horses. You'll ride, of course. You'll enjoy that. There's a horse over at Eglinton I'd like you to see. A beautiful animal, perfectly trained, no vice in him but plenty of spirit."

The car slowed down to take the turn into the gates of Kingsdean. Harry wrenched the wheel and swore as a grotesque figure sprang up in the middle of the road and he only just managed to avoid it. It stood there, shaking a fist and shouting after them.

Louise clutched his arm. "Who's that—that horrible old woman?"

Harry's brow was black. "That's old Murgatroyd. She and her husband were caretakers in the old house. They were there for nearly thirty years."

"Why does she shake her fist at you?"

Harry's face got red. "She—well, she resented the house being pulled down. And she got the sack, of course. Her husband's been dead two years. They say she got a bit queer after he died."

"Is she—she isn't—starving?"

Louise's ideas were vague and somewhat melodramatic. Riches prevented you coming into contact with reality.

Harry was outraged. "Good Lord, Louise, what an idea! I pensioned her off, of course—and handsomely, too! Found her a new cottage and everything."

Louise asked, bewildered, "Then why does she mind?"

Harry was frowning, his brows drawn together. "Oh, how should I know? Craziness! She loved the house."

"But it was a ruin, wasn't it?"

"Of course it was—crumbling to pieces—roof leaking —more or less unsafe. All the same I suppose it meant something to her. She's been there a long time. Oh, I don't know! The old devil's cracked, I think."

Louise said uneasily, "She—I think she cursed us. Oh, Harry, I wish she hadn't."

It seemed to Louise that her new home was tainted and poisoned by the malevolent figure of one crazy old woman. When she went out in the car, when she rode, when she walked out with the dogs, there was always the same figure waiting. Crouched down on herself, a battered hat over wisps of iron-gray hair, and the slow muttering of imprecations.

Louise came to believe that Harry was right—the old woman was mad. Nevertheless that did not make things easier. Mrs. Murgatroyd never actually came to the house, nor did she use definite threats, nor offer violence. Her squatting figure remained always just outside the gates. To appeal to the police would have been useless and, in any case, Harry Laxton was averse to that course of action. It would, he said, arouse local sympathy for the old brute. He took the matter more easily than Louise did.

"Don't worry about it, darling. She'll get tired of this silly cursing business. Probably she's only trying it on."

"She isn't, Harry. She—she hates us! I can feel it. She —she's ill-wishing us."

"She's not a witch, darling, although she may look like one! Don't be morbid about it all."

Louise was silent. Now that the first excitement of settling in was over, she felt curiously lonely and at a loose end. She had been used to life in London and the Riviera. She had no knowledge of or taste for English country life. She was ignorant of gardening, except for the final act of "doing the flowers." She did not really care for dogs. She was bored by such neighbors as she met. She enjoyed riding best, sometimes with Harry, sometimes, when he was busy about the estate, by herself. She hacked through the woods and lanes, enjoying the easy paces of the beautiful horse that Harry had bought for her. Yet even Prince Hal, most sensitive of chestnut steeds, was wont to shy and snort as he carried his mistress past that huddled figure of a malevolent old woman.

One day Louise took her courage in both hands. She was out walking. She had passed Mrs. Murgatroyd, pretending not to notice her, but suddenly she swerved back and went right up to her. She said, a little breathlessly, "What is it? What's the matter? What do you want?"

The old woman blinked at her. She had a cunning, dark gypsy face, with wisps of iron-gray hair, and bleared, suspicious eyes. Louise wondered if she drank.

She spoke in a whining and yet threatening voice. "What do I want, you ask? What, indeed! That which has been took away from me. Who turned me out of Kingsdean House? I'd lived there, girl and woman, for near on forty years. It was a black deed to turn me out and it's black bad luck it'll bring to you and him!"

Louise said, "You've got a very nice cottage and—"

She broke off. The old woman's arms flew up. She screamed, "What's the good of that to me? It's my own place I want and my own fire as I sat beside all them years. And as for you and him, I'm telling you there will be no happiness for you in your new fine house. It's the black sorrow will be upon you! Sorrow and death and my curse. May your fair face rot."

Louise turned away and broke into a little stumbling run. She thought, *I must get away from here! We must sell the house! We must go away.*

At the moment, such a solution seemed easy to her. But Harry's utter incomprehension took her aback. He exclaimed, "Leave here? Sell the house? Because of a crazy old woman's threats? You must be mad."

"No, I'm not. But she—she frightens me. I know something will happen."

Harry Luxton said grimly, "Leave Mrs. Murgatroyd to me. I'll settle her!"

A friendship had sprung up between Clarice Vane and young Mrs. Laxton. The two girls were much of an age, though dissimilar both in character and in tastes. In Clarice's company, Louise found reassurance. Clarice was so self-reliant, so sure of herself. Louise mentioned the matter of Mrs. Murgatroyd and her threats, but Clarice seemed to regard the matter as more annoying than frightening.

"It's so stupid, that sort of thing," she said. "And really very annoying for you."

"You know, Clarice, I—I feel quite frightened sometimes. My heart gives the most awful jumps."

"Nonsense, you mustn't let a silly thing like that get you down. She'll soon tire of it."

She was silent for a minute or two. Clarice said, "What's the matter?"

Louise paused for a minute, then her answer came with a rush. "I hate this place! I hate being here. The woods and this house, and the awful silence at night, and the queer noise owls make. Oh, and the people and everything."

"The people. What people?"

"The people in the village. Those prying, gossiping old maids."

Clarice said sharply, "What have they been saying?"

"I don't know. Nothing particular. But they've got nasty minds. When you've talked to them you feel you wouldn't trust anybody—not anybody at all."

Clarice said harshly, "Forget them. They've nothing to do but gossip. And most of the muck they talk they just invent."

Louise said, "I wish we'd never come here. But Harry adores it so." Her voice softened.

Clarice thought, *How she adores him.* She said abruptly, "I must go now."

"I'll send you back in the car. Come again soon."

Clarice nodded. Louise felt comforted by her new

friend's visit. Harry was pleased to find her more cheerful and from then on urged her to have Clarice often to the house.

Then one day he said, "Good news for you, darling."

"Oh, what?"

"I've fixed the Murgatroyd. She's got a son in America, you know. Well, I've arranged for her to go out and join him. I'll pay her passage."

"Oh, Harry, how wonderful. I believe I might get to like Kingsdean after all."

"Get to like it? Why, it's the most wonderful place in the world!"

Louise gave a little shiver. She could not rid herself of her superstitious fear so easily.

If the ladies of St. Mary Mead had hoped for the pleasure of imparting information about her husband's past to the bride, this pleasure was denied them by Harry Laxton's own prompt action.

Miss Harmon and Clarice Vane were both in Mr. Edge's shop, the one buying mothballs and the other a packet of boracic, when Harry Laxton and his wife came in.

After greeting the two ladies, Harry turned to the counter and was just demanding a toothbrush when he stopped in mid-speech and exclaimed heartily, "Well, well, just see who's here! Bella, I do declare."

Mrs. Edge, who had hurried out from the back parlor to attend to the congestion of business, beamed back cheerfully at him, showing her big white teeth. She had been a dark, handsome girl and was still a reasonably handsome woman, though she had put on weight, and the lines of her face had coarsened; but her large brown eyes were full of warmth as she answered, "Bella, it is, Mr. Harry, and pleased to see you after all these years."

Harry turned to his wife. "Bella's an old flame of mine, Louise," he said. "Head-over-ears in love with her, wasn't I, Bella?"

"That's what you say," said Mrs. Edge.

Louise laughed. She said, "My husband's very happy seeing all his old friends again."

"Ah," said Mrs. Edge, "we haven't forgotten you, Mr. Harry. Seems like a fairy tale to think of you married and building up a new house instead of that ruined old Kingsdean House."

"You look very well and blooming," said Harry, and Mrs. Edge laughed and said there was nothing wrong with her and what about that toothbrush?

Clarice, watching the baffled look on Miss Harmon's face, said to herself exultantly, *Oh, well done, Harry. You've spiked their guns.*

Doctor Haydock said abruptly to his niece, "What's all this nonsense about old Mrs. Murgatroyd hanging about Kingsdean and shaking her fist and cursing the new regime?"

"It isn't nonsense. It's quite true. It's upset Louise a good deal."

"Tell her she needn't worry—when the Murgatroyds were caretakers they never stopped grumbling about the place—they only stayed because Murgatroyd drank and couldn't get another job."

"I'll tell her," said Clarice doubtfully, "but I don't think she'll believe you. The old woman fairly screams with rage."

"Always used to be fond of Harry as a boy. I can't understand it."

Clarice said, "Oh, well—they'll be rid of her soon. Harry's paying her passage to America."

Three days later, Louise was thrown from her horse

and killed.

Two men in a baker's van were witnesses of the accident. They saw Louise ride out of the gates, saw the old woman spring up and stand in the road waving her arms and shouting, saw the horse start, swerve, and then bolt madly down the road, flinging Louise Laxton over his head.

One of them stood over the unconscious figure, not knowing what to do, while the other rushed to the house to get help.

Harry Laxton came running out, his face ghastly. They took off a door of the van and carried her on it to the house. She died without regaining consciousness and before the doctor arrived.

(End of Doctor Haydock's manuscript.)

When Doctor Haydock arrived the following day, he was pleased to note that there was a pink flush in Miss Marple's cheek and decidedly more animation in her manner.

"Well," he said, "what's the verdict?"

"What's the problem, Doctor Haydock?" countered Miss Marple.

"Oh, my dear lady, do I have to tell you that?"

"I suppose," said Miss Marple, "that it's the curious conduct of the caretaker. Why did she behave in that very odd way? People do mind being turned out of their old homes. But it wasn't her home. In fact, she used to complain and grumble while she was there. Yes, it certainly looks very fishy. What became of her, by the way?"

"Did a bunk to Liverpool. The accident scared her. Thought she'd wait there for her boat."

"All very convenient for somebody," said Miss Marple. "Yes, I think the 'Problem of the Caretaker's Conduct' can be solved easily enough. Bribery, was it not?"

"That's your solution?"

"Well, if it wasn't natural for her to behave in that way, she must have been 'putting on an act' as people say, and that means that somebody paid her to do what she did."

"And you know who that somebody was?"

"Oh, I think so. Money again, I'm afraid. And I've always noticed that gentlemen always tend to admire the same type."

"Now I'm out of my depth."

"No, no, it all hangs together. Harry Laxton admired Bella Edge, a dark, vivacious type. Your niece Clarice was the same. But the poor little wife was quite a different type—fair-haired and clinging—not his type at all. So he must have married her for her money. And murdered her for her money, too!"

"You use the word 'murder'?"

"Well, he sounds the right type. Attractive to women and quite unscrupulous. I suppose he wanted to keep his wife's money and marry your niece. He may have been seen talking to Mrs. Edge. But I don't fancy he was attached to her any more. Though I daresay he made the poor woman think he was, for ends of his own. He soon had her well under his thumb, I fancy."

"How exactly did he murder her, do you think?"

Miss Marple stared ahead of her for some minutes with dreamy blue eyes.

"It was very well timed—with the baker's van as witness. They could see the old woman and, of course, they'd put down the horse's fright to that. But I should imagine, myself, that an air gun, or perhaps a catapult—he used to be good with a catapult. Yes, just as the horse came through the gates. The horse bolted, of course, and Mrs. Laxton was thrown."

She paused, frowning.

"The fall might have killed her. But he couldn't be sure of that. And he seems the sort of man who would lay his plans carefully and leave nothing to chance. After all, Mrs. Edge could get him something suitable without her husband knowing. Otherwise, why would Harry bother with her? Yes, I think he had some powerful drug handy, that could be administered before you arrived. After all, if a woman is thrown from her horse and has serious injuries and dies without recovering consciousness, well—a doctor wouldn't normally be suspicious, would he? He'd put it down to shock or something."

Doctor Haydock nodded.

"Why did you suspect?" asked Miss Marple.

"It wasn't any particular cleverness on my part," said Doctor Haydock. "It was just the trite, well-known fact that a murderer is so pleased with his cleverness that he doesn't take proper precautions. I was just saying a few consolatory words to the bereaved husband—and feeling damned sorry for the fellow, too—when he flung himself down on the settee to do a bit of play-acting and a hypodermic syringe fell out of his pocket.

"He snatched it up and looked so scared that I began to think. Harry Laxton didn't drug; he was in perfect health; what was he doing with a hypodermic syringe? I did the autopsy with a view to certain possibilities. I found strophanthin. The rest was easy. There was strophanthin in Laxton's possession, and Bella Edge, questioned by the police, broke down and admitted to having got it for him. And finally old Mrs. Murgatroyd confessed that it was Harry Laxton who had put her up to the cursing stunt."

"And your niece got over it?"

"Yes, she was attracted by the fellow, but it hadn't gone far."

The doctor picked up his manuscript.

"Full marks to you, Miss Marple—and full marks to me for my prescription. You're looking almost yourself again."

The Third-Floor Flat

"BOTHER!" SAID PAT.

With a deepening frown she rummaged wildly in the silken trifle she called an evening bag. Two young men and another girl watched her anxiously. They were all standing outside the closed door of Patricia Garnett's flat.

"It's no good," said Pat. "It's not there. And now what shall we do?"

"What is life without a latchkey?" murmured Jimmy Faulkener.

He was a short, broad-shouldered young man, with good-tempered blue eyes.

Pat turned on him angrily. "Don't make jokes, Jimmy. This is serious."

"Look again, Pat," said Donovan Bailey. "It must be there somewhere."

He had a lazy, pleasant voice that matched his lean, dark figure.

"If you ever brought it out," said the other girl, Mildred Hope.

"Of course I brought it out," said Pat. "I believe I gave it to one of you two." She turned on the man accusingly. "I told Donovan to take it for me."

But she was not to find a scapegoat so easily. Donovan put in a firm disclaimer, and Jimmy backed him up.

"I saw you put it in your bag, myself," said Jimmy.

"Well, then, one of you dropped it out when you picked up my bag. I've dropped it once or twice."

"Once or twice!" said Donovan. "You've dropped it a dozen times at least, besides leaving it behind on every possible occasion."

"I can't see why everything on earth doesn't drop out of it the whole time," said Jimmy.

"The point is—how are we going to get in?" said Mildred.

She was a sensible girl, who kept to the point, but she was not nearly so attractive as the impulsive and troublesome Pat.

All four of them regarded the closed door blankly.

"Couldn't the porter help?" suggested Jimmy. "Hasn't he got a master key or something of that kind?"

Pat shook her head. There were only two keys. One was inside the flat hung up in the kitchen and the other was—or should be—in the maligned bag.

"If only the flat were on the ground floor," wailed Pat. "We could have broken open a window or something. Donovan, you wouldn't like to be a cat burglar, would you?"

Donovan declined firmly but politely to be a cat burglar.

"A flat on the fourth floor is a bit of an undertaking," said Jimmy.

"How about a fire escape?" suggested Donovan.

"There isn't one."

"There should be," said Jimmy. "A building five stories high ought to have a fire escape."

"I daresay," said Pat. "But what should be doesn't help us. How am I ever to get into my flat?"

"Isn't there a sort of thingummybob?" said Donovan. "A thing the tradesmen send up chops and Brussels sprouts in?"

"The service lift," said Pat. "Oh, yes, but it's only a sort of wire-basket thing. Oh! wait—I know. What about the coal lift?"

"Now that," said Donovan, "is an idea."

Mildred made a discouraging suggestion. "It'll be bolted," she said. "In Pat's kitchen, I mean, on the inside."

But the idea was instantly negatived.

"Don't you believe it," said Donovan.

"Not in *Pat's* kitchen," said Jimmy. "Pat never locks and bolts things."

"I don't think it's bolted," said Pat. "I took the dustbin off this morning, and I'm sure I never bolted it afterward, and I don't think I've been near it since."

"Well," said Donovan, "that fact's going to be very useful to us tonight, but, all the same, young Pat, let me point out to you that these slack habits are leaving you at the mercy of burglars—non-feline—every night."

Pat disregarded these admonitions.

"Come on," she cried, and began racing down the four flights of stairs. The others followed her. Pat led them through a dark recess, apparently full to overflowing of perambulators, and through another door into the well of the flats, and guided them to the right lift. There was, at the moment, a dustbin on it. Donovan lifted it off and stepped gingerly onto the platform in its place. He wrinkled up his nose.

"A little noisome," he remarked. "But what of that? Do I go alone on this venture or is anyone coming with me?"

"I'll come, too," said Jimmy.

He stepped on by Donovan's side.

"I suppose the lift will bear me," he added doubtfully.

"You can't weigh much more than a ton of coal," said Pat, who had never been particularly strong on her weights-and-measures table.

"And, anyway, we shall soon find out," said Donovan cheerfully, as he hauled on the rope.

With a grinding noise they disappeared from sight.

"This thing makes an awful noise," remarked Jimmy, as they passed up through blackness. "What will the people in the other flats think?"

"Ghosts or burglars, I expect," said Donovan. "Hauling this rope is quite heavy work. The porter of Friars Mansions does more work than I ever suspected. I say, Jimmy, old son, are you counting the floors?"

"Oh, Lord! No. I forgot about it."

"Well, I have, which is just as well. That's the third we're passing now. The next is ours."

"And now, I suppose," grumbled Jimmy, "we shall find that Pat did bolt the door after all."

But these fears were unfounded. The wooden door swung back at a touch, and Donovan and Jimmy stepped out into the inky blackness of Pat's kitchen.

"We ought to have a torch for this wild night work," explained Donovan. "If I know Pat, everything's on the floor, and we shall smash endless crockery before I can get to the light switch. Don't move about, Jimmy, till I get the light on."

He felt his way cautiously over the floor, uttering one fervent "Damn!" as a corner of the kitchen table took him unawares in the ribs. He reached the switch, and in another moment another "Damn!" floated out of the darkness.

"What's the matter?" asked Jimmy.

"Light won't come on. Dud bulb, I suppose. Wait a minute. I'll turn the sitting-room light on."

The sitting-room was the door immediately across the passage. Jimmy heard Donovan go out of the door, and presently fresh muffled curses reached him. He himself edged his way cautiously across the kitchen.

"What's the matter?"

"I don't know. Rooms get bewitched at night, I believe. Everything seems to be in a different place. Chairs and tables where you least expected them. Oh, hell! Here's another!"

But at this moment Jimmy fortunately connected with the electric-light switch and pressed it down. In another minute two young men were looking at each other in silent horror.

This room was not Pat's sitting-room. They were in the wrong flat.

To begin with, the room was about ten times more crowded than Pat's, which explained Donovan's pathetic bewilderment at repeatedly cannoning into chairs and tables. There was a large round table in the center of the room covered with a baize cloth, and there was an aspidistra in the window. It was, in fact, the kind of room whose owner, the young men felt sure, would be difficult to explain to. With silent horror they gazed down at the table, on which lay a little pile of letters.

"Mrs. Ernestine Grant," breathed Donovan, picking them up and reading the name. "Oh, help! Do you think she's heard us?"

"It's a miracle she hasn't heard you," said Jimmy. "What with your language and the way you've been crashing into the furniture. Come on, for the Lord's sake, let's get out of here quickly."

They hastily switched off the light and retraced their steps on tiptoe to the lift. Jimmy breathed a sigh of relief as they regained the fastness of its depths without further incident.

"I do like a woman to be a good, sound sleeper," he said approvingly. "Mrs. Ernestine Grant has her points."

"I see it now," said Donovan; "why we made the mistake in the floor, I mean. Out in that well we started up from the basement." He heaved on the rope, and the lift shot up. "We're right this time."

"I devoutly trust we are," said Jimmy as he stepped

out into another inky void. "My nerves won't stand many more shocks of this kind."

But no further nerve strain was imposed. The first click of the light showed them Pat's kitchen, and in another minute they were opening the front door and admitting the two girls who were waiting outside.

"You have been a long time," grumbled Pat. "Mildred and I have been waiting here ages."

"We've had an adventure," said Donovan. "We might have been hauled off to the police station as dangerous malefactors."

Pat had passed on into the sitting-room, where she switched on the light and dropped her wrap on the sofa. She listened with lively interest to Donovan's account of his adventures.

"I'm glad she didn't catch you," she commented. "I'm sure she's an old curmudgeon. I got a note from her this morning—wanted to see me sometime—something she had to complain about—my piano, I suppose. People who don't like pianos over their heads shouldn't come and live in flats. I say, Donovan, you've hurt your hand. It's all over blood. Go and wash it under the tap."

Donovan looked down at his hand in surprise. He went out of the room obediently and presently his voice called to Jimmy.

"Hullo," said the other, "what's up? You haven't hurt yourself badly, have you?"

"I haven't hurt myself at all."

There was something so queer in Donovan's voice that Jimmy stared at him in surprise. Donovan held out his washed hand and Jimmy saw that there was no mark or cut of any kind on it.

"That's odd," he said, frowning. "There was quite a lot of blood. Where did it come from?" And then suddenly he realized what his quicker-witted friend had already seen. "By Jove," he said. "It must have come from that flat." He stopped, thinking over the possibilities his words implied. "You're sure it was—er—blood?" he said. "Not paint?"

Donovan shook his head. "It was blood, all right," he said, and shivered.

They looked at each other. The same thought was clearly in each of their minds. It was Jimmy who voiced it first.

"I say," he said awkwardly. "Do you think we ought to—well—go down again—and have—a—a look around? See it's all right, you know?"

"What about the girls?"

"We won't say anything to them. Pat's going to put on an apron and make us an omelet. We'll be back by the time they wonder where we are."

"Oh, well, come on," said Donovan. "I suppose we've got to go through with it. I daresay there isn't anything really wrong."

But his tone lacked conviction. They got into the lift and descended to the floor below. They found their way across the kitchen without much difficulty and once more switched on the sitting-room light.

"It must have been in here," said Donovan, "that—that I got the stuff on me. I never touched anything in the kitchen."

He looked round him. Jimmy did the same, and they both frowned. Everything looked neat and commonplace and miles removed from any suggestion of violence or gore.

Suddenly Jimmy started violently and caught his companion's arm.

"Look!"

Donovan followed the pointing finger, and in his turn uttered an exclamation. From beneath the heavy rep curtains there protruded a foot—a woman's foot in a gaping patent-leather shoe.

Jimmy went to the curtains and drew them sharply apart. In the recess of the window a woman's huddled body lay on the floor, a sticky dark pool beside it. She was dead, there was no doubt of that. Jimmy was attempting to raise her up when Donovan stopped him.

"You'd better not do that. She oughtn't to be touched till the police come."

"The police. Oh! Of course. I say, Donovan, what a ghastly business. Who do you think she is? Mrs. Ernestine Grant?"

"Looks like it. At any rate, if there's anyone else in the flat they're keeping jolly quiet."

"What do we do next?" asked Jimmy. "Run out and get a policeman or ring up from Pat's flat?"

"I should think ringing up would be best. Come on, we might as well go out the front door. We can't spend the whole night going up and down in that evil-smelling lift."

Jimmy agreed. Just as they were passing through the door he hesitated. "Look here; do you think one of us ought to stay—just to keep an eye on things—till the police come?"

"Yes, I think you're right. If you'll stay I'll run up and telephone."

He ran quickly up the stairs and rang the bell of the flat above. Pat came to open it, a very pretty Pat with a flushed face and a cooking apron on. Her eyes widened in surprise.

"You? But how—Donovan, what is it? Is anything the matter?"

He took both her hands in his. "It's all right, Pat—only we've made rather an unpleasant discovery in the flat below. A woman—dead."

"Oh!" She gave a little gasp. "How horrible. Has she had a fit or something?"

"No. It looks—well—it looks rather as though she had been murdered."

"Oh, Donovan!"

"I know. It's pretty beastly."

Her hands were still in his. She had left them there—was even clinging to him. Darling Pat—how he loved her. Did she care at all for him? Sometimes he thought she did. Sometimes he was afraid that Jimmy Faulkener—remembrances of Jimmy waiting patiently below made him start guiltily.

"Pat, dear, we must telephone to the police."

"Monsieur is right," said a voice behind him. "And in the meantime, while we are waiting their arrival, perhaps I can be of some slight assistance."

They had been standing in the doorway of the flat, and now they peered out onto the landing. A figure was standing on the stairs a little way above them. It moved down and into their range of vision.

They stood staring at a little man with a very fierce mustache and an egg-shaped head. He wore a resplendent dressing-gown and embroidered slippers. He bowed gallantly to Patricia.

"Mademoiselle!" he said. "I am, as perhaps you know, the tenant of the flat above. I like to be up high—the air—the view over London. I take the flat in the name of Mr. O'Connor. But I am not an Irishman. I have another name. That is why I venture to put myself at your service. Permit me." With a flourish he pulled out a card and handed it to Pat. She read it.

"M. Hercule Poirot. Oh!" She caught her breath. *"The* M. Poirot? The great detective? And you will really help?"

"That is my intention, mademoiselle. I nearly offered

my help earlier in the evening."

Pat looked puzzled.

"I heard you discussing how to gain admission to your flat. Me, I am very clever at picking locks. I could, without doubt, have opened your door for you, but I hesitated to suggest it. You would have had the grave suspicions of me."

Pat laughed.

"Now, monsieur," said Poirot to Donovan. "Go in, I pray of you, and telephone to the police. I will descend to the flat below."

Pat came down the stairs with him. They found Jimmy on guard, and Pat explained Poirot's presence. Jimmy, in his turn, explained to Poirot his and Donovan's adventures. The detective listened attentively.

"The lift door was unbolted, you say? You emerged into the kitchen, but the light it would not turn on."

He directed his footsteps to the kitchen as he spoke. His fingers pressed the switch.

"*Tiens! Voilà ce qui est curieux!*" he said as the light flashed on. "It functions perfectly now. I wonder—"

He held up a finger to insure silence and listened. A faint sound broke the stillness—the sound of an unmistakable snore.

"Ah!" said Poirot. "*La chambre de domestique.*"

He tiptoed across the kitchen into a little pantry, out of which led a door. He opened the door and switched on the light. The room was the kind of dog kennel designed by the builders of flats to accommodate a human being. The floor space was almost entirely occupied by the bed. In the bed was a rosy-cheeked girl lying on her back with her mouth wide-open, snoring placidly.

Poirot switched off the light and beat a retreat.

"She will not wake," he said. "We will let her sleep till the police come."

He went back to the sitting-room. Donovan had joined them.

"The police will be here almost immediately, they say," he said breathlessly. "We are to touch nothing."

Poirot nodded. "We will not touch," he said. "We will look, that is all."

He moved into the room. Mildred had come down with Donovan, and all four young people stood in the doorway and watched him with breathless interest.

"What I can't understand, sir, is this," said Donovan. "I never went near the window—how did the blood come on my hand?"

"My young friend, the answer to that stares you in the face. Of what color is the tablecloth? Red, is it not? and doubtless you did put your hand on the table."

"Yes, I did. Is that—" He stopped.

Poirot nodded. He was bending over the table. He indicated with his hand a dark patch on the red.

"It was here that the crime was committed," he said solemnly. "The body was moved afterward."

Then he stood upright and looked slowly round the room. He did not move, he handled nothing, but nevertheless the four watching felt as though every object in that rather frowsty place gave up its secret to his observant eye.

Hercule Poirot nodded his head as though satisfied. A little sigh escaped him. "I see," he said.

"You see what?" asked Donovan curiously.

"I see," said Poirot, "what you doubtless felt—that the room is overfull of furniture."

Donovan smiled ruefully. "I did go barging about a bit," he confessed. "Of course, everything was in a different place to Pat's room, and I couldn't make it out."

"Not everything," said Poirot.

Donovan looked at him inquiringly.

"I mean," said Poirot apologetically, "that certain things are always fixed. In a block of flats the door, the window, the fireplace—they are in the same place in the rooms which are below each other."

"Isn't that rather splitting hairs?" asked Mildred. She was looking at Poirot with faint disapproval.

"One should always speak with absolute accuracy. That is a little—how do you say?—fad of mine."

There was the noise of footsteps on the stairs, and three men came in. They were a police inspector, a constable, and the divisional surgeon. The inspector recognized Poirot and greeted him in an almost reverential manner. Then he turned to the others.

"I shall want statements from everyone," he began, "but in the first place—"

Poirot interrupted. "A little suggestion. We will go back to the flat upstairs and mademoiselle here shall do what she was planning to do—make us an omelet. Me, I have a passion for the omelets. Then, *M. l'Inspecteur*, when you have finished here, you will mount to us and ask questions at your leisure."

It was arranged accordingly, and Poirot went up with them.

"M. Poirot," said Pat, "I think you're a perfect dear. And you shall have a lovely omelet. I really make omelets frightfully well."

"That is good. Once, mademoiselle, I loved a beautiful young English girl, who resembled you greatly—but alas! —she could not cook. So perhaps everything was for the best."

There was a faint sadness in his voice, and Jimmy Faulkener looked at him curiously.

Once in the flat, however, he exerted himself to please and amuse. The grim tragedy below was almost forgotten.

The omelet had been consumed and duly praised by the time that Inspector Rice's footsteps were heard. He came in accompanied by the doctor, having left the constable below.

"Well, Monsieur Poirot," he said. "It all seems clear and aboveboard—not much in your line, though we may find it hard to catch the man. I'd just like to hear how the discovery came to be made."

Donovan and Jimmy between them recounted the happenings of the evening. The inspector turned reproachfully to Pat.

"You shouldn't leave your lift door unbolted, miss. You really shouldn't."

"I shan't again," said Pat, with a shiver. "Somebody might come in and murder me like that poor woman below."

"Ah! but they didn't come in that way, though," said the inspector.

"You will recount to us what you have discovered, yes?" said Poirot.

"I don't know as I ought to—but seeing it's you, M. Poirot—"

"*Précisément,*" said Poirot. "And these young people—they will be discreet."

"The newspapers will get hold of it, anyway, soon enough," said the inspector. "There's no real secret about the matter. Well, the dead woman's Mrs. Grant, all right. I had the porter up to identify her. Woman of about thirty-five. She was sitting at the table, and she was shot with an automatic pistol of small caliber, probably by someone sitting opposite her at table. She fell forward, and that's how the bloodstain came on the table."

"But wouldn't someone have heard the shot?" asked Mildred.

"The pistol was fitted with a silencer. No, you wouldn't hear anything. By the way, did you hear the screech the maid let out when we told her her mistress was dead? No. Well, that just shows how unlikely it was that anyone would hear the other."

"Has the maid no story to tell?" asked Poirot.

"It was her evening out. She's got her own key. She came in about ten o'clock. Everything was quiet. She thought her mistress had gone to bed."

"She did not look in the sitting-room, then?"

"Yes, she took the letters in there which had come by the evening post, but she saw nothing unusual—any more than Mr. Faulkener and Mr. Bailey did. You see, the murderer had concealed the body rather neatly behind the curtains."

"But it was a curious thing to do, don't you think?"

Poirot's voice was very gentle, yet it held something that made the inspector look up quickly.

"Didn't want the crime discovered till he'd had time to make his getaway."

"Perhaps—perhaps— But continue with what you were saying."

"The maid went out at five o'clock. The doctor here puts the time of death as—roughly—about four to five hours ago. That's right, isn't it?"

The doctor, who was a man of few words, contented himself with jerking his head affirmatively.

"It's a quarter to twelve now. The actual time can, I think, be narrowed down to a fairly definite hour."

He took out a crumpled sheet of paper.

"We found this in the pocket of the dead woman's dress. You needn't be afraid of handling it. There are no fingerprints on it."

Poirot smoothed out the sheet. Across it some words were printed in small, prim capitals.

I WILL COME TO SEE YOU THIS EVENING AT HALF PAST SEVEN.—J. F.

"A compromising document to leave behind," commented Poirot, as he handed it back.

"Well, he didn't know she'd got it in her pocket," said the inspector. "He probably thought she'd destroyed it. We've evidence that he was a careful man, though. The pistol she was shot with we found under the body—and there again no fingerprints. They'd been wiped off very carefully with a silk handkerchief."

"How do you know," said Poirot, "that it was a silk handkerchief?"

"Because we found it," said the inspector triumphantly. "At the last, as he was drawing the curtains, he must have let it fall unnoticed."

He handed across a big white silk handkerchief—a good-quality handkerchief. It did not need the inspector's finger to draw Poirot's attention to the mark on it in the center. It was neatly marked and quite legible. Poirot read the name out.

"John Fraser."

"That's it," said the inspector. "John Fraser—J. F. in the note. We know the name of the man we have to look for, and I daresay when we find out a little about the dead woman, and her relations come forward, we shall soon get a line on him."

"I wonder," said Poirot. "No, *mon cher,* somehow I do not think he will be easy to find, your John Fraser. He is a strange man—careful, since he marks his handkerchiefs and wipes the pistol with which he has committed the crime—yet careless since he loses his handkerchief and does not search for a letter that might incriminate him."

"Flurried, that's what he was," said the inspector.

"It is possible," said Poirot. "Yes, it is possible. And he was not seen entering the building?"

"There are all sorts of people going in and out at that time. These are big blocks. I suppose none of you"—he addressed the four collectively—"saw anyone coming out of the flat?"

Pat shook her head. "We went out earlier—about seven o'clock."

"I see." The inspector rose. Poirot accompanied him to the door.

"As a little favor, may I examine the flat below?"

"Why, certainly, M. Poirot. I know what they think of you at headquarters. I'll leave you a key. I've got two. It will be empty. The maid cleared out to some relatives, too scared to stay there alone."

"I thank you," said M. Poirot. He went back into the flat, thoughtful.

"You're not satisfied, M. Poirot?" said Jimmy.

"No," said Poirot. "I am not satisfied."

Donovan looked at him curiously. "What is it that—well, worries you?"

Poirot did not answer. He remained silent for a minute or two, frowning, as though in thought, then he made a sudden impatient movement of shoulders.

"I will say good night to you, mademoiselle. You must be tired. You have had much cooking to do—eh?"

Pat laughed. "Only the omelet. I didn't do dinner. Donovan and Jimmy came and called for us, and we went out to a little place in Soho."

"And then without doubt, you went to a theater?"

"Yes. 'The Brown Eyes of Caroline.'"

"Ah!" said Poirot. "It should have been blue eyes—the blue eyes of mademoiselle."

He made a sentimental gesture, and then once more wished Pat good night, also Mildred, who was staying the night by special request, as Pat admitted frankly that she would get the horrors if left alone on this particular night.

The two young men accompanied Poirot. When the door was shut, and they were preparing to say good-by to him on the landing, Poirot forestalled them.

"My young friends, you heard me say that I was not satisfied? *Eh bien,* it is true—I am not. I go now to make some little investigations of my own. You would like to accompany me—yes?"

An eager assent greeted this proposal. Poirot led the way to the flat below and inserted the key the inspector had given him in the lock. On entering, he did not, as the others had expected, enter the sitting-room. Instead he went straight to the kitchen. In a little recess which served as a scullery a big iron bin was standing. Poirot uncovered this and, doubling himself up, began to rootle in it with the energy of a ferocious terrier.

Both Jimmy and Donovan stared at him in amazement.

Suddenly with a cry of triumph he emerged. In his hand he held aloft a small stoppered bottle.

"*Voilà!*" he said. "I find what I seek." He sniffed at it delicately. "Alas! I am *enrhumé*—I have the cold in the head."

Donovan took the bottle from him and sniffed in his turn, but could smell nothing. He took out the stopper and held the bottle to his nose before Poirot's warning cry could stop him.

Immediately he fell like a log. Poirot, by springing forward, partly broke his fall.

"Imbecile!" he cried. "The idea. To remove the stopper in that foolhardy manner! Did he not observe how delicately I handled it? Monsieur—Faulkener—is it not? Will you be so good as to get me a little brandy? I observed a decanter in the sitting-room."

Jimmy hurried off, but by the time he returned, Donovan was sitting up and declaring himself quite all right again. He had to listen to a short lecture from Poirot on the necessity of caution in sniffing at possibly poisonous substances.

"I think I'll be off home," said Donovan, rising shakily to his feet. "That is, if I can't be any more use here. I feel a bit wonky still."

"Assuredly," said Poirot. "That is the best thing you can do. M. Faulkener, attend me here a little minute. I will return on the instant."

He accompanied Donovan to the door and beyond. They remained outside on the landing talking for some minutes. When Poirot at last re-entered the flat he found Jimmy standing in the sitting-room gazing round him with puzzled eyes.

"Well, M. Poirot," he said, "what next?"

"There is nothing next. The case is finished."

"What?"

"I know everything—now."

Jimmy stared at him. "That little bottle you found?"

"Exactly. That little bottle."

Jimmy shook his head. "I can't make head or tail of it. For some reason or other I can see you are dissatisfied with the evidence against this John Fraser, whoever he may be."

"Whoever he may be," repeated Poirot softly. "If he is anyone at all—well, I shall be surprised."

"I don't understand."

"He is a name—that is all—a name carefully marked on a handkerchief!"

"And the letter?"

"Did you notice that it was printed? Now, why? I will tell you. Handwriting might be recognized, and a type-written letter is more easily traced than you would im-agine—but if a real John Fraser wrote that letter those two points would not have appealed to him! No, it was written on purpose, and put in the dead woman's pocket for us to find. There is no such person as John Fraser."

Jimmy looked at him inquiringly.

"And so," went on Poirot, "I went back to the point that first struck me. You heard me say that certain things in a room were always in the same place under given circumstances. I gave three instances. I might have mentioned a fourth—the electric-light switch, my friend."

Jimmy still stared uncomprehendingly. Poirot went on.

"Your friend Donovan did not go near the window— it was by resting his hand on this table that he got it covered in blood! But I asked myself at once—why did he rest it there? What was he doing groping about this room in darkness? For remember, my friend, the electric-light switch is always in the same place—by the door. Why, when he came to this room, did he not at once feel for the light and turn it on? That was the natural, the normal thing to do. According to him, he tried to turn on the light in the kitchen, but failed. Yet when I tried the switch it was in perfect working order. Did he, then, not wish the light to go on just then? If it had gone on you would both have seen at once that you were in the wrong flat. There would have been no reason to come into this room."

"What are you driving at, M. Poirot? I don't understand. What do you mean?"

"I mean—this."

Poirot held up a Yale door key.

"The key of this flat?"

"No, *mon ami*, the key of the flat above. Mademoiselle Patricia's key, which M. Donovan Bailey abstracted from her bag sometime during the evening."

"But why—why?"

"*Parbleu!* so that he could do what he wanted to do

—gain admission to this flat in a perfectly unsuspicious manner. He made sure that the lift door was unbolted earlier in the evening."

"Where did you get the key?"

Poirot's smile broadened. "I found it just now—where I looked for it—in M. Donovan's pocket. See you, that little bottle I pretended to find was a ruse. M. Donovan is taken in. He does what I knew he would do—unstoppers it and sniffs. And in that little bottle is ethyl chloride, a very powerful instant anesthetic. It gives me just the moment or two of unconsciousness I need. I take from his pocket the two things that I knew would be there. This key was one of them—the other—"

He stopped and then went on.

"I questioned at the time the reason the inspector gave for the body being concealed behind the curtain. To gain time? No, there was more than that. And so I thought of just one thing—the post, my friend. The evening post that comes at half past nine or thereabouts. Say the murderer does not find something he expects to find, but that something may be delivered by post later. Clearly, then, he must come back. But the crime must not be discovered by the maid when she comes in, or the police would take possession of the flat, so he hides the body behind the curtain. And the maid suspects nothing and lays the letters on the table as usual."

"The letters?"

"Yes, the letters." Poirot drew something from his pocket. "This is the second article I took from M. Donovan when he was unconscious." He showed the superscription—a typewritten envelope addressed to Mrs. Ernestine Grant. "But I will ask you one thing first, M. Faulkener, before we look at the contents of this letter. Are you or are you not in love with Mademoiselle Patricia?"

"I care for Pat damnably—but I've never thought I had a chance."

"You thought that she cared for M. Donovan? It may be that she had begun to care for him—but it was only a beginning, my friend. It is for you to make her forget—to stand by her in her trouble."

"Trouble?" said Jimmy sharply.

"Yes, trouble. We will do all we can to keep her name out of it, but it will be impossible to do so entirely. She was, you see, the motive."

He ripped open the envelope that he held. An enclosure fell out. The covering letter was brief, and was from a firm of solicitors.

Dear Madam,

The document you enclose is quite in order, and the fact of the marriage having taken place in a foreign country does not invalidate it in any way.

Yours truly, etc.

Poirot spread out the enclosure. It was a certificate of marriage between Donovan Bailey and Ernestine Grant, dated eight years ago.

"Oh, my God!" said Jimmy. "Pat said she'd had a letter from the woman asking to see her, but she never dreamed it was anything important."

Poirot nodded. "M. Donovan knew—he went to see his wife this evening before going to the flat above—a strange irony, by the way, that led the unfortunate woman to come to this building where her rival lived—he murdered her in cold blood—and then went on to his evening's amusement. His wife must have told him that she had sent the marriage certificate to her solicitors and was expecting to hear from them. Doubtless he himself had tried to make her believe that there was a flaw in the marriage."

"He seemed in quite good spirits, too, all the evening. M. Poirot, you haven't let him escape?" Jimmy shuddered.

"There is no escape for him," said Poirot gravely. "You need not fear."

"It's Pat I'm thinking about mostly," said Jimmy. "You don't think—she really cared."

"*Mon ami,* that is your part," said Poirot gently. "To make her turn to you and forget. I do not think you will find it very difficult!"

The Adventure of Johnnie Waverly

"You can understand the feelings of a mother," said Mrs. Waverly for perhaps the sixth time.

She looked appealingly at Poirot. My little friend, always sympathetic to motherhood in distress, gesticulated reassuringly.

"But yes, but yes, I comprehend perfectly. Have faith in Papa Poirot."

"The police—" began Mr. Waverly.

His wife waved the interruption aside. "I won't have anything more to do with the police. We trusted to them and look what happened! But I'd heard so much of M. Poirot and the wonderful things he'd done, that I felt he might possibly be able to help us. A mother's feelings—"

Poirot hastily stemmed the reiteration with an eloquent gesture. Mrs. Waverly's emotion was obviously genuine, but it assorted strangely with her shrewd, rather hard type of countenance. When I heard later that she was the daughter of a prominent steel manufacturer of Birmingham who had worked his way up in the world from an office boy to his present eminence, I realized that she had inherited many of the paternal qualities.

Mr. Waverly was a big, florid, jovial-looking man. He stood with his legs straddled wide apart and looked the type of the country squire.

"I suppose you know all about this business, M. Poirot?"

The question was almost superfluous. For some days past the paper had been full of the sensational kidnaping of little Johnnie Waverly, the three-year-old son and heir of Marcus Waverly, Esq., of Waverly Court, Surrey, one of the oldest families in England.

"The main facts I know, of course, but recount to me the whole story, monsieur, I beg of you. And in detail if you please."

"Well, I suppose the beginning of the whole thing was about ten days ago when I got an anonymous letter—beastly things, anyway—that I couldn't make head or tail of. The writer had the impudence to demand that I should pay him twenty-five thousand pounds—twenty-five thousand pounds, M. Poirot! Failing my agreement, he threatened to kidnap Johnnie. Of course I threw the thing into the wastepaper basket without more ado. Thought it was some silly joke. Five days later I got another letter. 'Unless you pay, your son will be kidnaped on the twenty-ninth.' That was on the twenty-seventh. Ada was worried, but I couldn't bring myself to treat the matter seriously. Damn it all, we're in England. Nobody goes about kidnaping children and holding them up to ransom."

"It is not a common practice, certainly," said Poirot. "Proceed, monsieur."

"Well, Ada gave me no peace, so—feeling a bit of a fool—I laid the matter before Scotland Yard. They didn't seem to take the thing very seriously—inclined to my view that it was some silly joke. On the twenty-eighth I got a third letter. 'You have not paid. Your son will be taken from you at twelve o'clock noon tomorrow, the twenty-ninth. It will cost you fifty thousand pounds to recover him.' Up I drove to Scotland Yard again. This time they were more impressed. They inclined to the view that the letters were written by a lunatic, and that in all probability an attempt of some kind would be made at the hour stated. They assured me that they would take all due precautions. Inspector McNeil and a sufficient force would come down to Waverly on the norrow and take charge.

"I went home much relieved in my mind. Yet we already had the feeling of being in a state of siege. I gave orders that no stranger was to be admitted, and that no one was to leave the house. The evening passed off without any untoward incident, but on the following morning my wife was seriously unwell. Alarmed by her condition, I sent for Doctor Dakers. Her symptoms appeared to puzzle him. While hesitating to suggest that she had been poisoned, I could see that that was what was in his mind. There was no danger, he assured me, but it would be a day or two before she would be able to get about again. Returning to my own room, I was startled and amazed to find a note pinned to my pillow. It was in the same handwriting as the others and contained just three words: 'At twelve o'clock.'

"I admit, M. Poirot, that then I saw red! Someone in the house was in this—one of the servants. I had them all up, blackguarded them right and left. They never split on each other; it was Miss Collins, my wife's companion, who informed me that she had seen Johnnie's nurse slip down the drive early that morning. I taxed her with it, and she broke down. She had left the child with the nursery maid and stolen out to meet a friend of hers—a man! Pretty goings on! She denied having pinned the note to my pillow—she may have been speaking the truth, I don't know. I felt I couldn't take the risk of the child's own nurse being in the plot. One of the servants was implicated—of that I was sure. Finally I lost my temper and sacked the whole bunch, nurse and all. I gave them an hour to pack their boxes and get out of the house."

Mr. Waverly's red face was quite two shades redder as he remembered his just wrath.

"Was not that a little injudicious, monsieur?" suggested Poirot. "For all you know, you might have been playing into the enemy's hands."

Mr. Waverly stared at him. "I don't see that. Send the whole lot packing, that was my idea. I wired to London for a fresh lot to be sent down that evening. In the meantime, there'd be only people I could trust in the house, my wife's secretary, Miss Collins, and Tredwell, the butler, who has been with me since I was a boy."

"And this Miss Collins, how long has she been with you?"

"Just a year," said Mrs. Waverly. "She has been invaluable to me as a secretary-companion, and is also a very efficient housekeeper."

"The nurse?"

"She has been with me six months. She came to me with excellent references. All the same I never really liked her, although Johnnie was quite devoted to her."

"Still, I gather she had already left when the catastrophe occurred. Perhaps, Monsieur Waverly, you will be so kind as to continue."

Mr. Waverly resumed his narrative.

"Inspector McNeil arrived about ten-thirty. The servants had all left by then. He declared himself quite satisfied with the internal arrangements. He had various men posted in the park outside, guarding all the approaches to the house, and he assured me that if the whole thing were not a hoax, we should undoubtedly catch my mysterious correspondent.

"I had Johnnie with me, and he and I and the inspector went together into a room we call the Council Chamber. The inspector locked the door. There is a big grandfather clock there, and as the hands drew near to twelve I don't mind confessing that I was as nervous as a cat. There was a whirring sound, and the clock began to strike. I clutched Johnnie. I had a feeling a man might drop from the skies. The last stroke sounded, and as it did so, there was a great commotion outside—shouting and running. The inspector flung up the window, and a constable came running up.

" 'We've got him, sir,' he panted. 'He was sneaking up through the bushes. He's got a whole dope outfit on him.'

"We hurried out on the terrace where two constables were holding a ruffianly-looking fellow in shabby clothes, who was twisting and turning in a vain endeavor to escape. One of the policemen held out an unrolled parcel which they had wrested from their captive. It contained a pad of cotton wool and a bottle of chloroform. It made my blood boil to see it. There was a note, too, addressed to me. I tore it open. It bore the following words: 'You should have paid up. To ransom your son will now cost you fifty thousand. In spite of all your precautions he has been abducted at twelve o'clock on the twenty-ninth as I said.'

"I gave a great laugh, the laugh of relief, but as I did so I heard the hum of a motor and a shout. I turned my head. Racing down the drive toward the south lodge at a furious speed was a low, long gray car. It was the man who drove it who had shouted, but that was not what gave me a shock of horror. It was the sight of Johnnie's flaxen curls. The child was in the car beside him.

"The inspector ripped out an oath.

" 'The child was here not a minute ago,' he cried. His eyes swept over us. We were all there, myself, Tredwell, Miss Collins. 'When did you see him last, Mr. Waverly?'

"I cast my mind back, trying to remember. When the constable had called us, I had run out with the inspector, forgetting all about Johnnie.

"And then there came a sound that startled us, the

chiming of a church clock from the village. With an exclamation the inspector pulled out his watch. It was exactly twelve o'clock. With one common accord we ran to the Council Chamber, the clock there marked the hour as ten minutes past. Someone must have deliberately tampered with it, for I have never known it gain or lose before. It is a perfect timekeeper."

Mr. Waverly paused. Poirot smiled to himself and straightened a little mat which the anxious father had pushed askew.

"A pleasing little problem, obscure and charming," murmured Poirot. "I will investigate it for you with pleasure. Truly it was planned *à merveille*."

Mrs. Waverly looked at him reproachfully. "But my boy," she wailed.

Poirot hastily composed his face and looked the picture of earnest sympathy again. "He is safe, madame, he is unharmed. Rest assured, these miscreants will take the greatest care of him. Is he not to them the turkey—no, the goose—that lays the golden eggs?"

"M. Poirot, I'm sure there's only one thing to be done —pay up. I was all against it at first—but now! A mother's feelings—"

"But we have interrupted monsieur in his history," cried Poirot hastily.

"I expect you know the rest pretty well from the papers," said Mr. Waverly. "Of course, Inspector McNeil got onto the telephone immediately. A description of the car and the man was circulated all round, and it looked at first as though everything was going to turn out all right. A car, answering to the description, with a man and a small boy, had passed through various villages, apparently making for London. At one place they had stopped, and it was noticed that the child was crying and obviously afraid of his companion. When Inspector Mc-

Neil announced that the car had been stopped and the man and boy detained, I was almost ill with relief. You know the sequel. The boy was not Johnnie, and the man was an ardent motorist, fond of children, who had picked up a small child playing in the streets of Edenswell, a village about fifteen miles from us, and was kindly giving him a ride. Thanks to the cocksure blundering of the police, all traces have disappeared. Had they not persistently followed the wrong car, they might by now have found the boy."

"Calm yourself, monsieur. The police are a brave and intelligent force of men. Their mistake was a very natural one. And altogether it was a clever scheme. As to the man they caught in the grounds, I understand that his defense has consisted all along of a persistent denial. He declares that the note and parcel were given to him to deliver at Waverly Court. The man who gave them to him handed him a ten-shilling note and promised him another if it were delivered at exactly ten minutes to twelve. He was to aproach the house through the grounds and knock at the side door."

"I don't believe a word of it," declared Mrs. Waverly hotly. "It's all a parcel of lies."

"*En vérité,* it is a thin story," said Poirot reflectively. "But so far they have not shaken it. I understand, also, that he made a certain accusation?"

His glance interrogated Mr. Waverly. The latter got rather red again.

"The fellow had the impertinence to pretend that he recognized in Tredwell the man who gave him the parcel. 'Only the bloke has shaved off his mustache.' Tredwell, who was born on the estate!"

Poirot smiled a little at the country gentleman's indignation. "Yet you yourself suspect an inmate of the house to have been accessory to the abduction."

"Yes, but not Tredwell."

"And you, madame?" asked Poirot, suddenly turning to her.

"It could not have been Tredwell who gave this tramp the letter and parcel—if anybody ever did, which I don't believe— It was given him at ten o'clock, he says. At ten o'clock, Tredwell was with my husband in the smoking-room."

"Were you able to see the face of the man in the car, monsieur? Did it resemble that of Tredwell in any way?"

"It was too far away for me to see his face."

"Has Tredwell a brother, do you know?"

"He had several, but they are all dead. The last one was killed in the war."

"I am not yet clear as to the grounds of Waverly Court. The car was heading for the south lodge. Is there another entrance?"

"Yes, what we call the east lodge. It can be seen from the other side of the house."

"It seems to me strange that nobody saw the car entering the grounds."

"There is a right of way through, and access to a small chapel. A good many cars pass through. The man must have stopped the car in a convenient place and run up to the house just as the alarm was given and attention attracted elsewhere."

"Unless he was already inside the house," mused Poirot. "Is there any place where he could have hidden?"

"Well, we certainly didn't make a thorough search of the house beforehand. There seemed no need. I suppose he might have hidden himself somewhere, but who would have let him in?"

"We shall come to that later. One thing at a time— let us be methodical. There is no special hiding-place in the house? Waverly Court is an old place, and there are sometimes 'priest's holes' as they call them."

"By gad, there *is* a priest's hole. It opens from one of the panels in the hall."

"Near the Council Chamber?"

"Just outside the door."

"*Voilà!*"

"But nobody knows of its existence except my wife and myself."

"Tredwell?"

"Well—he might have heard of it."

"Miss Collins?"

"I have never mentioned it to her."

Poirot reflected for a minute.

"Well, monsieur, the next thing is for me to come down to Waverly Court. If I arrive this afternoon, will it suit you?"

"Oh, as soon as possible, please, Monsieur Poirot!" cried Mrs. Waverly. "Read this once more."

She thrust into his hands the last missive from the enemy which had reached the Waverlys that morning and which had sent her posthaste to Poirot. It gave clever and explicit directions for the paying over of the money, and ended with a threat that the boy's life would pay for any treachery. It was clear that a love of money warred with the essential mother love of Mrs. Waverly, and that the latter was at last gaining the day.

Poirot detained Mrs. Waverly for a minute behind her husband.

"Madame, the truth, if you please. Do you share your husband's faith in the butler, Tredwell?"

"I have nothing against him, Monsieur Poirot, I cannot see how he can have been concerned in this, but—well, I have never liked him—never!"

"One other thing, madame, can you give me the address of the child's nurse?"

"149 Netherall Road, Hammersmith. You don't imagine—"

"Never do I imagine. Only—I employ the little gray cells. And sometimes, just sometimes, I have a little idea."

Poirot came back to me as the door closed.

"So madame has never liked the butler. It is interesting, that, eh, Hastings?"

I refused to be drawn. Poirot has deceived me so often that I now go warily. There is always a catch somewhere.

After completing an elaborate outdoor toilet, we set off for Netherall Road. We were fortunate enough to find Miss Jessie Withers at home. She was a pleasant-faced woman of thirty-five, capable and superior. I could not believe that she could be mixed up in the affair. She was bitterly resentful of the way she had been dismissed, but admitted that she had been in the wrong. She was engaged to be married to a painter and decorator who happened to be in the neighborhood, and she had run out to meet him. The thing seemed natural enough. I could not quite understand Poirot. All his questions seemed to me quite irrelevant. They were concerned mainly with the daily routine of her life at Waverly Court. I was frankly bored and glad when Poirot took his departure.

"Kidnaping is an easy job, *mon ami*," he observed, as he hailed a taxi in the Hammersmith Road and ordered it to drive to Waterloo. "That child could have been abducted with the greatest ease any day for the last three years."

"I don't see that that advances us much," I remarked coldly.

"*Au contraire*, it advances us enormously, but enormously! If you must wear a tie pin, Hastings, at least let it be in the exact center of your tie. At present it is at least a sixteenth of an inch too much to the right."

Waverly Court was a fine old place and had recently been restored with taste and care. Mr. Waverly showed us the Council Chamber, the terrace, and all the various spots connected with the case. Finally, at Poirot's request, he pressed a spring in the wall, a panel slid aside, and a short passage led us into the priest's hole.

"You see," said Waverly. "There is nothing here."

The tiny room was bare enough, there was not even the mark of a footstep on the floor. I joined Poirot where he was bending attentively over a mark in the corner.

"What do you make of this, my friend?"

There were four imprints close together.

"A dog," I cried.

"A very small dog, Hastings."

"A Pom."

"Smaller than a Pom."

"A griffon?" I suggested doubtfully.

"Smaller even than a griffon. A species unknown to the Kennel Club."

I looked at him. His face was alight with excitement and satisfaction.

"I was right," he murmured. "I knew I was right. Come, Hastings."

As we stepped out into the hall and the panel closed behind us, a young lady came out of a door farther down the passage. Mr. Waverly presented her to us.

"Miss Collins."

Miss Collins was about thirty years of age, brisk and alert in manner. She had fair, rather dull hair, and wore pince-nez.

At Poirot's request, we passed into a small morning room, and he questioned her closely as to the servants and particularly as to Tredwell. She admitted that she did not like the butler.

"He gives himself airs," she explained.

They then went into the question of the food eaten by Mrs. Waverly on the night of the 28th. Miss Collins declared that she had partaken of the same dishes upstairs in her sitting-room and had felt no ill effects. As she was departing I nudged Poirot.

"The dog," I whispered.

"Ah, yes, the dog!" He smiled broadly. "Is there a dog kept here by any chance, mademoiselle?"

"There are two retrievers in the kennels outside."

"No, I mean a small dog, a toy dog."

"No—nothing of the kind."

Poirot permitted her to depart. Then, pressing the bell, he remarked to me, "She lies, that Mademoiselle Collins. Possibly I should, also, in her place. Now for the butler."

Tredwell was a dignified individual. He told his story with perfect aplomb, and it was essentially the same as that of Mr. Waverly. He admitted that he knew the secret of the priest's hole.

When he finally withdrew, pontifical to the last, I met Poirot's quizzical eyes.

"What do you make of it all, Hastings?"

"What do you?" I parried.

"How cautious you become. Never, never will the gray cells function unless you stimulate them. Ah, but I will not tease you! Let us make our deductions together. What points strike us specially as being difficult?"

"There is one thing that strikes me," I said. "Why did the man who kidnaped the child go out by the south lodge instead of by the east lodge where no one would see him?"

"That is a very good point, Hastings, an excellent one. I will match it with another. Why warn the Waverlys beforehand? Why not simply kidnap the child and hold him to ransom?"

"Because they hoped to get the money without being forced to action."

"Surely it was very unlikely that the money would be paid on a mere threat?"

"Also they wanted to focus attention on twelve o'clock, so that when the tramp man was seized, the other could emerge from his hiding-place and get away with the child unnoticed."

"That does not alter the fact that they were making a thing difficult that was perfectly easy. If they do not specify a time or date, nothing would be easier than to wait their chance, and carry off the child in a motor one day when he is out with his nurse."

"Ye—es," I admitted doubtfully.

"In fact, there is a deliberate playing of the farce! Now let us approach the question from another side. Everything goes to show that there was an accomplice inside the house. Point number one, the mysterious poisoning of Mrs. Waverly. Point number two, the letter pinned to the pillow. Point number three, the putting on of the clock ten minutes—all inside jobs. And an additional fact that you may not have noticed. There was no dust in the priest's hole. It had been swept out with a broom.

"Now, then, we have four people in the house. We can exclude the nurse, since she could not have swept out the priest's hole, though she could have attended to the other three points. Four people. Mr. and Mrs. Waverly, Tredwell, the butler, and Miss Collins. We will take Miss Collins first. We have nothing much against her, except that we know very little about her, that she is obviously an intelligent young woman, and that she has only been here a year."

"She lied about the dog, you said," I reminded him.

"Ah, yes, the dog." Poirot gave a peculiar smile. "Now let us pass to Tredwell. There are several suspicious facts against him. For one thing, the tramp declares that it was Tredwell who gave him the parcel in the village."

"But Tredwell can prove an alibi on that point."

"Even then, he could have poisoned Mrs. Waverly, pinned the note to the pillow, put on the clock, and swept out the priest's hole. On the other hand, he has been born and bred in the service of the Waverlys. It seems unlikely in the last degree that he should connive at the abduction of the son of the house. It is not in the picture!"

"Well, then?"

"We must proceed logically—however absurd it may seem. We will briefly consider Mrs. Waverly. But she is rich, the money is hers. It is her money which has restored this impoverished estate. There would be no reason for her to kidnap her son and pay over her money to herself. Her husband, now, is in a different position. He has a rich wife. It is not the same thing as being rich himself—in fact I have a little idea that the lady is not very fond of parting with her money, except on a very good pretext. But Mr. Waverly, you can see at once, he is *bon viveur*."

"Impossible," I spluttered.

"Not at all. Who sends away the servants? Mr. Waverly. He can write the notes, drug his wife, put on the hands of the clock, and establish an excellent alibi for his faithful retainer Tredwell. Tredwell has never liked Mrs. Waverly. He is devoted to his master and is willing to obey his orders implicitly. There were three of them in it. Waverly, Tredwell, and some friend of Waverly. That is the mistake the police made, they made no further inquiries about the man who drove the gray car with the wrong child in it. He was the third man. He picks up a child in a village near by, a boy with flaxen curls. He drives in through the east lodge and passes out through the south lodge just at the right moment, waving his hand and shouting. They cannot see his face or the number of the car, so obviously they cannot see the child's face, either. Then he lays a false trail to London. In the meantime, Tredwell has done his part in arranging for the parcel and note to be delivered by a rough-looking gentleman. His master can provide an alibi in the unlikely case of the man recognizing him, in spite of the false mustache he wore. As for Mr. Waverly, as soon as the hullabaloo occurs outside, and the inspector rushes out, he quickly hides the child in the priest's hole, and follows him out. Later in the day, when the inspector is gone and Miss Collins is out of the way, it will be easy enough to drive him off to some safe place in his own car."

"But what about the dog?" I asked. "And Miss Collins lying?"

"That was my little joke. I asked her if there were any toy dogs in the house, and she said no—but doubtless there are some—in the nursery! You see, Mr. Waverly placed some toys in the priest's hole to keep Johnnie amused and quiet."

"M. Poirot." Mr. Waverly entered the room. "Have you discovered anything? Have you any clue to where the boy has been taken?"

Poirot handed him a piece of paper. "Here is the address."

"But this is a blank sheet."

"Because I am waiting for you to write it down for me."

"What the—" Mr. Waverly's face turned purple.

"I know everything, monsieur. I give you twenty-four hours to return the boy. Your ingenuity will be equal to the task of explaining his reappearance. Otherwise, Mrs. Waverly will be informed of the exact sequence of events."

Mr. Waverly sank down in a chair and buried his face in his hands. "He is with my old nurse, ten miles away. He is happy and well cared for."

"I have no doubt of that. If I did not believe you to be a good father at heart, I should not be willing to give you another chance."

"The scandal—"

"Exactly. Your name is an old and honored one. Do not jeopardize it again. Good evening, Mr. Waverly. Ah! by the way, one word of advice. Always sweep in the corners!"

Four and Twenty Blackbirds

HERCULE POIROT WAS DINING with his friend, Henry Bonnington, at the Gallant Endeavor in the King's Road, Chelsea.

Mr. Bonnington was fond of the Gallant Endeavor. He liked the leisurely atmosphere, he liked the food which was "plain" and "English" and "not a lot of made-up messes."

Molly, the sympathetic waitress, greeted him as an old friend. She prided herself on remembering her customers' likes and dislikes in the way of food.

"Good evening, sir," she said as the two men took their seats at a corner table. "You're in luck today—turkey stuffed with chestnuts—that's your favorite, isn't it? And ever such a nice Stilton we've got! Will you have soup first or fish?"

The question of food and wine settled, Mr. Bonnington leaned back with a sigh and unfolded his napkin as Molly sped away.

"Good girl, that!" he said approvingly. "Was quite a beauty once—artists used to paint her. She knows about food, too—and that's a great deal more important. Women are very unsound on food as a rule. There's many a woman, if she goes out with a fellow she fancies, won't even notice what she eats. She'll just order the first thing she sees."

Hercule Poirot shook his head. *"C'est terrible."*

"Men aren't like that, thank goodness!" said Mr. Bonnington complacently.

"Never?" There was a twinkle in Hercule Poirot's eye.

"Well, perhaps when they're very young," conceded Mr. Bonnington. "Young puppies! Young fellows nowadays are all the same—no guts—no stamina. I've no use for the young—and they," he added with strict impartiality, "have no use for me. Perhaps they're right! But to hear some of these young fellows talk you'd think no man had a right to be *alive* after sixty! From the way they go on, you'd wonder more of them didn't help their elderly relations out of the world."

"It is possible," said Hercule Poirot, "that they do."

"Nice mind you've got, Poirot, I must say. All this police work saps your ideals."

Hercule Poirot smiled. "Nevertheless," he said, "it would be interesting to make a table of accidental deaths over the age of sixty. I assure you it would raise some curious speculations in your mind. But tell me, my friend, of your own affairs. How does the world go with you?"

"Mess!" said Mr. Bonnington. "That's what's the matter with the world nowadays. Too much mess. And too much fine language. The fine language helps to conceal the mess. Like a highly flavored sauce concealing the fact that the fish underneath it is none of the best! Give me an honest fillet of sole and no messy sauce over it."

It was given him at that moment by Molly, and he grunted approval.

"You know just what I like, my girl," he said.

"Well, you come here pretty regular, don't you, sir? So I ought to know."

Hercule Poirot said, "Do people, then, always like the same things? Do not they like a change sometimes?"

"Not gentlemen, sir. Ladies like variety—gentlemen always like the same thing."

"What did I tell you?" grunted Bonnington. "Women are fundamentally unsound where food is concerned!"

He looked around the restaurant.

"The world's a funny place. See that odd-looking old fellow with a beard in the corner? Molly'll tell you he's always here Tuesday and Thursday nights. He has come here for close on ten years now—he's a kind of landmark in the place. Yet nobody here knows his name or where he lives or what his business is. It's odd when you come to think of it."

When the waitress brought the portions of turkey he said, "I see you've still got Old Father Time over there."

"That's right, sir. Tuesdays and Thursdays, his days are. Not but what he came in here on a *Monday* last week! It quite upset me! I felt I'd got my dates wrong and that it must be Tuesday without my knowing it! But he came in the next night as well—so the Monday was just a kind of extra, so to speak."

"An interesting deviation from habit," murmured Poirot. "I wonder what the reason was?"

"Well, sir, if you ask me, I think he'd had some kind of upset or worry."

"Why did you think that? His manner?"

"No, sir—not his manner exactly. He was very quiet as he always is. Never says much except 'Good evening' when he comes and goes. No, it was his *order*."

"His order?"

"I daresay you gentlemen will laugh at me." Molly flushed. "But when a gentleman has been here for ten years, you get to know his likes and dislikes. He never could bear suet pudding or blackberries, and I've never known him to take thick soup—but on that Monday night he ordered thick tomato soup, beefsteak and kidney pudding, and blackberry tart! Seemed as though he just didn't notice *what* he ordered!"

"Do you know," said Hercule Poirot, "I find that extraordinarily interesting."

Molly looked gratified and departed.

"Well, Poirot," said Henry Bonnington with a chuckle. "Let's have a few deductions from you. All in your best manner."

"I would prefer to hear yours, first."

"Want me to be Watson, eh? Well, old fellow went to a doctor, and the doctor changed his diet."

"To thick tomato soup, steak and kidney pudding, and blackberry tart? I cannot imagine any doctor doing that."

"Don't you believe it, old boy. Doctors will put you onto anything."

"That is the only solution that occurs to you?"

Henry Bonnington said, "Well, seriously, I suppose there's only one explanation possible. Our unknown friend was in the grip of some powerful mental emotion. He was so perturbed by it that he literally did not notice what he was ordering or eating." He paused a minute, and then said, "You'll be telling me next that you know just *what* was on his mind. You'll say, perhaps, that he was making up his mind to commit a murder."

He laughed at his own suggestion.

Hercule Poirot did not laugh.

He has admitted that at that moment he was seriously worried. He claims that he ought then to have had some inkling of what was likely to occur.

His friends assure him that such an idea is quite fantastic.

It was some three weeks later that Hercule Poirot and Bonnington met again—this time their meeting was in the subway.

They nodded to each other, swaying about, hanging onto adjacent straps. Then at Piccadilly Circus there was a general exodus, and they found seats right at the forward end of the car—a peaceful spot, since nobody passed in or out that way.

"By the way," said Mr. Bonnington. "Do you remember that old boy we noticed at the Gallant Endeavor? I shouldn't wonder if he'd hopped it to a better world. He's not been there for a whole week. Molly's quite upset about it."

Hercule Poirot sat up. His eyes flashed.

"Indeed?" he said. "Indeed?"

Bonnington said, "D'you remember I suggested he'd been to a doctor and been put on a diet? Diet's nonsense, of course—but I shouldn't wonder if he had consulted a doctor about his health and what the doctor said gave him a bit of a jolt. That would account for him ordering things off the menu without noticing what he was doing. Quite likely the jolt he got hurried him out of the world sooner than he would have gone otherwise. Doctors ought to be careful what they tell a chap."

"They usually are," said Hercule Poirot.

"This is my station," said Mr. Bonnington. "By-by. Don't suppose we shall ever know now who the old boy was—not even his name. Funny world!"

He hurried out of the carriage.

Hercule Poirot, sitting frowning, looked as though he did not think it was such a funny world. He went home and gave certain instructions to his faithful valet, George.

Hercule Poirot ran his finger down a list of names. It was a record of deaths within a certain area.

Poirot's finger stopped.

"Henry Gascoigne. Sixty-nine. I might try him first."

Later in the day Hercule Poirot was sitting in Dr. MacAndrew's surgery just off the King's Road. Mac-

Andrew was a tall, red-haired Scotsman with an intelligent face.

"Gascoigne?" he said. "Yes, that's right. Eccentric old bird. Lived alone in one of those derelict old houses that are being cleared away in order to build a block of modern flats. I hadn't attended him before, but I'd seen him about and I knew who he was. It was the dairy people got the wind up first. The milk bottles began to pile up outside. In the end the people next door sent word to the police, and they broke the door in and found him. He'd pitched down the stairs and broken his neck. Had on an old dressing-gown with a ragged cord—might easily have tripped himself up with it."

"I see," said Hercule Poirot. "It was quite simple—an accident."

"That's right."

"Had he any relations?"

"There's a nephew. Used to come along and see his uncle about once a month. Ramsey, his name is, George Ramsey. He's a medico himself. Lives at Wimbledon."

"How long had Mr. Gascoigne been dead when you saw him?"

"Ah!" said Dr. MacAndrew. "This is where we get official. Not less than forty-eight hours and not more than seventy-two hours. He was found on the morning of the sixth. Actually, we got closer than that. He had a letter in the pocket of his dressing-gown—written on the third—posted in Wimbledon that afternoon—would have been delivered somewhere around nine-twenty p.m. That puts the time of death at after nine-twenty on the evening of the third. That agrees with the contents of the stomach and the processes of digestion. He had had a meal about two hours before death. I examined him on the morning of the sixth, and his condition was quite consistent with death having occurred about sixty hours previously—around about ten p.m. on the third."

"It all seems very consistent. Tell me, when was he last seen alive?"

"He was seen in the King's Road about seven o'clock that same evening, Thursday the third, and he dined at the Gallant Endeavor restaurant at seven-thirty. It seems he always dined there on Thursdays."

"He had no other relations? Only this nephew?"

"There was a twin brother. The whole story is rather curious. They hadn't seen each other for years. As a young man Henry was by way of being an artist, you know. An extremely bad one. It seems the other brother, Anthony Gascoigne, married a very rich woman and gave up art—and the brothers quarreled over it. Hadn't seen each other since, I believe. But oddly enough, *they died on the same day.* The elder twin passed away at one o'clock on the afternoon of the third. Once before I've known a case of twins dying on the same day—in different parts of the world! Probably just a coincidence—but there it is."

"Is the other brother's wife alive?"

"No, she died some years ago."

"Where did Anthony Gascoigne live?"

"He had a house on Kingston Hill. He was, I believe, from what Doctor Ramsey tells me, very much of a recluse."

Hercule Poirot nodded thoughtfully.

The Scotsman looked at him keenly. "What exactly have you got in your mind, M. Poirot?" he asked bluntly. "I've answered your questions—as was my duty, seeing the credentials you brought. But I'm in the dark as to what it's all about."

Poirot said slowly, "A simple case of accidental death, that's what you said. What I have in mind is equally simple—a simple push."

Dr. MacAndrew looked startled.

"In other words, murder! Have you any grounds for that belief?"

"No," said Poirot. "It is a mere supposition."

"There must be something—" persisted the other.

Poirot did not speak.

MacAndrew said, "If it's the nephew, Ramsey, you suspect, I don't mind telling you here and now that you are barking up the wrong tree. Ramsey was playing bridge in Wimbledon from eight-thirty till midnight. That came out at the inquest."

Poirot murmured, "And presumably it was verified. The police are careful."

The doctor said, "Perhaps you know something against him?"

"I didn't know that there was such a person until you mentioned him."

"Then you suspect somebody else?"

"No, no. It is not that at all. It's a case of the routine habits of the human animal. That is very important. And the dead M. Gascoigne does not fit in. It is all wrong, you see."

"I really don't understand."

Hercule Poirot smiled. He rose, and the doctor rose, also.

"You know," said MacAndrew, "honestly, I can't see anything the least bit suspicious about the death of Henry Gascoigne."

The little man spread out his hands. "I'm an obstinate man—a man with a little idea—and nothing to support it! By the way, Doctor MacAndrew, did Henry Gascoigne have false teeth?"

"No, his own teeth were in excellent preservation. Very creditable indeed at his age."

"He looked after them well—they were white and well-brushed?"

"Yes, I noticed them particularly."

"Not discolored in any way?"

"No. I don't think he was a smoker if that is what you mean."

"I did not mean that precisely—it was just a long shot —which probably will not come off! Good-by, Doctor MacAndrew, and thank you for your kindness."

He shook the doctor's hand and departed.

"And now," he said, "for the long shot."

At the Gallant Endeavor, he sat down at the same table that he had shared with Bonnington. The girl who served him was not Molly. Molly, the girl told him, was away on a holiday.

It was just seven, and Hercule Poirot found no difficulty in entering into conversation with the girl on the subject of old Mr. Gascoigne.

"Yes," she said. "He'd been here for years and years. But none of us girls ever knew his name. We saw about the inquest in the paper, and there was a picture of him. 'There,' I said to Molly, 'if that isn't our Old Father Time,' as we used to call him."

"He dined here on the evening of his death, did he not?"

"That's right. Thursday, the third. He was always here on a Thursday. Tuesdays and Thursdays—punctual as a clock."

"You don't remember, I suppose, what he had for dinner?"

"Now let me see, it was mulligatawny soup, that's right, and beefsteak pudding, or was it the mutton? No, pudding, that's right, and blackberry-and-apple pie and cheese. And then to think of him going home and falling down those stairs that very same evening. A frayed dressing-gown cord they said it was as caused it. Of course, his clothes were always something awful—old-fashioned and put on anyhow, and all tattered, and yet he *had* a kind of air, all the same, as though he was *somebody!* Oh, we get all sorts of interesting customers here."

She moved off.

Hercule Poirot ate his sole.

Armed with introductions from a certain influential quarter, Hercule Poirot found no difficulty at all in dealing with the coroner for the district.

"A curious figure, the deceased man Gascoigne," he observed. "A lonely, eccentric old fellow. But his decease seems to arouse an unusual amount of attention." He looked with some curiosity at his visitor as he spoke.

Hercule Poirot chose his words carefully. "There are circumstances connected with it, monsieur, which make investigation desirable."

"Well, how can I help you?"

"It is, I believe, within your province to order documents produced in your court to be destroyed, or to be impounded—as you think fit. A certain letter was found in the pocket of Henry Gascoigne's dressing-gown, was it not?"

"That is so."

"A letter from his nephew, Doctor George Ramsey?"

"Quite correct. The letter was produced at the inquest as helping to fix the time of death."

"Is that letter still available?"

Hercule Poirot waited rather anxiously for the reply. When he heard that the letter was still available for examination he drew a sigh of relief. When it was finally produced he studied it with some care. It was written in a slightly cramped handwriting with a stylographic pen. It ran as follows:

Dear Uncle Henry:

I am sorry to tell you that I have had no success as regards Uncle Anthony. He showed no enthusiasm for a visit from you and would give me no reply to your request that he would let bygones be bygones. He is, of course, extremely ill, and his mind is inclined to wander. I should fancy that the end is very near. He seemed hardly to remember who you were.

I am sorry to have failed you, but I can assure you that I did my best.

Your affectionate nephew,
George Ramsey.

The letter itself was dated 3d November. Poirot glanced at the envelope's postmark—4:30 p.m.

He murmured, "It is beautifully in order, is it not?"

Kingston Hill was his next objective. After a little trouble, with the exercise of good-humored pertinacity, he obtained an interview with Amelia Hill, cook-housekeeper to the late Anthony Gascoigne.

Mrs. Hill was inclined to be stiff and suspicious at first, but the charming geniality of this strange-looking foreigner soon had its effect. Mrs. Amelia Hill began to unbend.

She found herself, as had so many other women before her, pouring out her troubles to a really sympathetic listener.

For fourteen years she had had charge of Mr. Gascoigne's household—*not* an easy job! No, indeed! Many a woman would have quailed under the burdens *she* had to bear! Eccentric the poor gentleman was and no denying it. Remarkably close with his money—a kind of mania with him it was—and he as rich a gentleman as might be! But Mrs. Hill had served him faithfully and put up with his ways, and naturally she'd expected at any rate a *remembrance*. But no—nothing at all! Just an old will that left all his money to his wife and if she predeceased him then everything to his brother, Henry. A will made years ago. It didn't seem fair!

Gradually Hercule Poirot detached her from her main theme of unsatisfied cupidity. It was indeed a heartless injustice! Mrs. Hill could not be blamed for feeling hurt and surprised. It was well known that Mr. Gascoigne was tightfisted about money. It had even been said that the dead man had refused his only brother assistance. Mrs. Hill probably knew all about that.

"Was it that that Doctor Ramsey came to see him about?" asked Mrs. Hill. "I knew it was something about his brother, but I thought it was just that his brother wanted to be reconciled. They'd quarreled years ago."

"I understand," said Poirot, "that Mr. Gascoigne refused absolutely?"

"That's right enough," said Mrs. Hill with a nod. " 'Henry?' he says, rather weaklike. 'What's this about Henry? Haven't seen him for years and don't want to. Quarrelsome fellow, Henry.' Just that."

The conversation then reverted to Mrs. Hill's own special grievances, and the unfeeling attitude of the late Mr. Gascoigne's solicitor.

With some difficulty Hercule Poirot took his leave without breaking off the conversation too abruptly.

And so, just after the dinner hour, he came to Elmcrest, Dorset Road, Wimbledon, the residence of Dr. George Ramsey.

The doctor was in. Hercule Poirot was shown into the surgery and there presently Dr. George Ramsey came to him, obviously just risen from the dinner table.

"I'm not a patient, doctor," said Hercule Poirot. "And my coming here is, perhaps, somewhat of an impertinence

—but I believe in plain and direct dealing. I do not care for lawyers and their long-winded, roundabout methods."

He had certainly aroused Ramsey's interest. The doctor was a clean-shaven man of middle height. His hair was brown, but his eyelashes were almost white, which gave his eyes a pale, boiled appearance. His manner was brisk and not without humor.

"Lawyers?" he said raising his eyebrows. "Hate the fellows! You rouse my curiosity, my dear sir. Pray sit down."

Poirot did so and then produced one of his professional cards which he handed to the doctor. George Ramsey's white eyelashes blinked.

Poirot leaned forward confidentially. "A good many of my clients are women," he said.

"Naturally," said Dr. George Ramsey, with a slight twinkle.

"As you say, naturally," agreed Poirot. "Women distrust the official police. They prefer private investigations. They do not want to have their troubles made public. An elderly woman came to consult me a few days ago. She was unhappy about a husband she'd quarreled with many years before. This husband of hers was your uncle, the late Mr. Gascoigne."

George Ramsey's face went purple. "My uncle? Nonsense! His wife died many years ago."

"Not your uncle, Mr. *Anthony* Gascoigne. Your uncle, Mr. *Henry* Gascoigne."

"Uncle Henry? But *he* wasn't married!"

"Oh, yes, he was," said Hercule Poirot, lying unblushingly. "Not a doubt of it. The lady even brought along her marriage certificate."

"It's a lie!" cried George Ramsey. His face was now as purple as a plum. "I don't believe it. You're an impudent liar."

"It is too bad, is it not?" said Poirot. "You have committed murder for nothing."

"Murder?" Ramsey's voice quavered. His pale eyes bulged with terror.

"By the way," said Poirot, "I see you have been eating blackberry tart again. An unwise habit. Blackberries are said to be full of vitamins, but they may be deadly in other ways. On this occasion I rather fancy they have helped to put a rope around a man's neck—your neck, Doctor Ramsey."

"You see, *mon ami,* where you went wrong was over your fundamental assumption." Hercule Poirot, beaming placidly across the table at his friend, waved an expository hand. "A man under severe mental stress doesn't choose that time to do something that he's never done before. His reflexes just follow the track of least resistance. A man who is upset about something *might* conceivably come down to dinner dressed in his pajamas— but they will be his *own* pajamas—not somebody else's.

"A man who dislikes thick soup, suet pudding, and blackberries suddenly orders all three one evening. *You* say because he is thinking of something else. But *I* say *that a man who has got something on his mind will order automatically the dish he has ordered most often before.*

"*Eh bien,* then, what other explanation could there be? I simply could not think of a reasonable explanation. And I was worried! The incident was all wrong.

"Then you told me that the man had disappeared. He had missed a Tuesday and a Thursday the first time for years. I liked that even less. A queer hypothesis sprang up in my mind. If I were right about it *the man was dead.* I made inquiries. The man *was* dead. And he was very neatly and tidily dead. In other words the bad fish was covered up with the sauce!

"He had been seen in the King's Road at seven o'clock. He had had dinner here at seven-thirty—two hours before he died. It all fitted in—the evidence of the stomach contents, the evidence of the letter. Much too much sauce! You couldn't see the fish at all!

"Devoted nephew wrote the letter, devoted nephew had beautiful alibi for time of death. Death very simple—a fall down the stairs. Simple accident? Or murder? Everyone says the former.

"Devoted nephew only surviving relative. Devoted nephew will inherit—but is there anything *to* inherit? Uncle notoriously poor.

"But there is a brother. And brother in his time had married a rich wife. And brother lives in a big rich house on Kingston Hill, so it would seem that rich wife must have left him all her money. You see the sequence—rich wife leaves money to Anthony, Anthony leaves money to Henry, Henry's money goes to George—a complete chain."

"All very pretty in theory," said Mr. Bonnington. "But what did you do?"

"Once you *know*—you can usually get hold of what you want. Henry had died two hours after a *meal*—that is all the inquest really bothered about. But supposing that meal was not dinner, but *lunch*. Put yourself in George's place. George wants money—badly. Anthony Gascoigne is dying—but his death is no good to George. His money goes to Henry, and Henry Gascoigne may live for years. So Henry must die, too—and the sooner the better—but his death must take place *after* Anthony's, and at the same time George must have an alibi. Henry's habit of dining regularly at a restaurant on two evenings of the week suggests an alibi to George. Being a cautious fellow, he tries his plan out first. *He impersonates his uncle one Monday evening at the restaurant in question.*

"It goes without a hitch. Everyone there accepts him as his uncle. He is satisfied. He has only to wait till Uncle Anthony shows definite signs of pegging out. The time comes. He mails a letter to his uncle on the afternoon of the second of November but dates it the third. He comes up to town on the afternoon of the third, calls on his uncle, and carries his scheme into action. A sharp shove and down the stairs goes Uncle Henry.

"George hunts about for the letter he has written, and shoves it in the pocket of his uncle's dressing-gown. At seven-thirty he is at the Gallant Endeavor, beard, bushy eyebrows, all complete. Undoubtedly Mr. Henry Gascoigne is alive at seven-thirty. Then a rapid metamorphosis in a lavatory and back full speed in his car to Wimbledon and an evening of bridge. The perfect alibi."

Mr. Bonnington looked at him. "But the postmark on the letter?"

"Oh, that was very simple. The postmark was smudgy. Why? It had been altered with lampblack from November second to November third. You would not notice it *unless you were looking for it.* And finally there were the blackbirds."

"Blackbirds?"

"Four-and-twenty blackbirds baked in a pie! Or blackberries if you prefer to be literal! George, you comprehend, was, after all, not quite a good enough actor. He *looked* like his uncle and *walked* like his uncle and *spoke* like his uncle and had his uncle's beard and eyebrows, but he forgot to *eat* like his uncle. He ordered the dishes that he himself liked.

"Blackberries discolor the teeth. The corpse's teeth were not discolored, and yet Henry Gascoigne ate blackberries at the Gallant Endeavor that night. But there were no blackberries in the stomach. I asked this morning. And George had been fool enough to keep the beard and the rest of the make-up. Oh! Plenty of evidence once you look for it. I called on George and rattled him. That finished it! He had been eating blackberries again, by the way. A greedy fellow—cared a lot about his food. *Eh bien,* greed will hang him, all right, unless I am very much mistaken."

A waitress brought them two portions of blackberry-and-apple tart.

"Take it away," said Mr. Bonnington. "One can't be too careful. Bring me a small helping of sago pudding."

The Love Detectives

LITTLE MR. SATTERTHWAITE LOOKED thoughtfully across at his host. The friendship between these two men was an odd one. The colonel was a simple country gentleman whose passion in life was sport. The few weeks that he spent perforce in London, he spent unwillingly. Mr. Satterthwaite, on the other hand, was a town bird. He was an authority on French cooking, on ladies' dress, and on all the latest scandals. His passion was observing human nature, and he was an expert in his own special line—that of an onlooker at life.

It would seem, therefore, that he and Colonel Melrose would have little in common, for the colonel had no interest in his neighbors' affairs and a horror of any kind of emotion. The two men were friends mainly because their fathers before them had been friends. Also they knew the same people and had reactionary views about *nouveaux riches.*

It was about half past seven. The two men were sitting in the colonel's comfortable study, and Melrose was describing a run of the previous winter with a keen hunting man's enthusiasm. Mr. Satterthwaite, whose knowledge of horses consisted chiefly of the time-honored Sunday-morning visit to the stables which still obtains in old-fashioned country houses, listened with his invariable politeness.

The sharp ringing of the telephone interrupted Melrose. He crossed to the table and took up the receiver.

"Hello, yes—Colonel Melrose speaking. What's that?"

His whole demeanor altered—became stiff and official.
was the magistrate speaking now, not the sportsman.
He listened for some moments, then said laconically,
ight, Curtis. I'll be over at once." He replaced the re-
ver and turned to his guest. "Sir James Dwighton has
n found in his library—murdered."

"What?"

Mr. Satterthwaite was startled—thrilled.

"I must go over to Alderway at once. Care to come
h me?"

Mr. Satterthwaite remembered that the colonel was
ef constable of the county.

"If I shan't be in the way—" He hesitated.

"Not at all. That was Inspector Curtis telephoning.
od, honest fellow, but no brains. I'd be glad if you
uld come with me, Satterthwaite. I've got an idea this
going to turn out a nasty business."

"Have they got the fellow who did it?"

"No," replied Melrose shortly.

Mr. Satterthwaite's trained ear detected a nuance of
erve behind the curt negative. He began to go over
his mind all that he knew of the Dwightons.

A pompous old fellow, the late Sir James, brusque in
s manner. A man that might easily make enemies. Veer-
g on sixty, with grizzled hair and a florid face. Reputed
be tightfisted in the extreme.

His mind went on to Lady Dwighton. Her image
ated before him, young, auburn-haired, slender. He
membered various rumors, hints, odd bits of gossip.
 that was it—that was why Melrose looked so glum.
en he pulled himself up—his imagination was running
ay with him.

Five minutes later Mr. Satterthwaite took his place
side his host in the latter's little two seater, and they
ove off together into the night.

The colonel was a taciturn man. They had gone qu[...]
a mile and a half before he spoke. Then he jerked [...]
abruptly, "You know 'em, I suppose?"

"The Dwightons? I know all about them, of cours[...]
Who was there Mr. Satterthwaite didn't know all abo[...]
"I've met him once, I think, and her rather oftener."

"Pretty woman," said Melrose.

"Beautiful!" declared Mr. Satterthwaite.

"Think so?"

"A pure Renaissance type," declared Mr. Satterthwai[...]
warming up to his theme. "She acted in those theatric[...]
—the charity matinee, you know, last spring. I was ve[...]
much struck. Nothing modern about her—a pure s[...]
vival. One can imagine her in the doge's palace, or [...]
Lucrezia Borgia."

The colonel let the car swerve slightly, and Mr. S[...]
terthwaite came to an abrupt stop. He wondered wh[...]
fatality had brought the name of Lucrezia Borgia to h[...]
tongue. Under the circumstances—

"Dwighton was not poisoned, was he?" he asked a[...]
ruptly.

Melrose looked at him sideways, somewhat curious[...]
"Why do you ask that, I wonder?" he said.

"Oh, I—I don't know." Mr. Satterthwaite was flustere[...]
"I— It just occurred to me."

"Well, he wasn't," said Melrose gloomily. "If you wa[...]
to know, he was crashed on the head."

"With a blunt instrument," murmured Mr. Satte[...]
thwaite, nodding his head sagely.

"Don't talk like a damned detective story, Satte[...]
thwaite. He was hit on the head with a bronze figure."

"Oh," said Satterthwaite, and relapsed into silence.

"Know anything of a chap called Paul Delangua[...]
asked Melrose after a minute or two.

"Yes. Good-looking young fellow."

"I daresay women would call him so," growled the
Colonel.

"You don't like him?"

"No, I don't."

"I should have thought you would have. He rides very
well."

"Like a foreigner at the horse show. Full of monkey
tricks."

Mr. Satterthwaite suppressed a smile. Poor old Melrose
was so very British in his outlook. Agreeably conscious
himself of a cosmopolitan point of view, Mr. Satterthwaite was able to deplore the insular attitude toward
life.

"Has he been down in this part of the world?" he
asked.

"He's been staying at Alderway with the Dwightons.
The rumor goes that Sir James kicked him out a week
ago."

"Why?"

"Found him making love to his wife, I suppose. What
the hell—"

There was a violent swerve, and a jarring impact.

"Most dangerous crossroads in England," said Melrose.
"All the same, the other fellow should have sounded his
horn. We're on the main road. I fancy we've damaged
him rather more than he has damaged us."

He sprang out. A figure alighted from the other car
and joined him. Fragments of speech reached Satterthwaite.

"Entirely my fault, I'm afraid," the stranger was saying. "But I do not know this part of the country very
well, and there's absolutely no sign of any kind to show
you're coming onto the main road."

The colonel, mollified, rejoined suitably. The two men
went together over the stranger's car, which a chauffeur

was already examining. The conversation became high
technical.

"A matter of half an hour, I'm afraid," said the stra
ger. "But don't let me detain you. I'm glad your c
escaped injury as well as it did."

"As a matter of fact—" the colonel was beginning, b
he was interrupted.

Mr. Satterthwaite, seething with excitement, hoppe
out of the car with a birdlike action, and seized th
stranger warmly by the hand.

"It is! I thought I recognized the voice," he declare
excitedly. "What an extraordinary thing. What a ve
extraordinary thing."

"Eh?" said Colonel Melrose.

"Mr. Harley Quin. Melrose, I'm sure you've heard m
speak many times of Mr. Quin?"

Colonel Melrose did not seem to remember the fac
but he assisted politely at the scene while Mr. Satte
thwaite was chirruping gaily on. "I haven't seen you
let me see—"

"Since the night at the Bells and Motley," said th
other quietly.

"The Bells and Motley, eh?" said the colonel.

"An inn," explained Mr. Satterthwaite.

"What an odd name for an inn."

"Only an old one," said Mr. Quin. "There was a tim
remember, when bells and motley were more common i
England than they are nowadays."

"I suppose so; yes, no doubt you are right," said Me
rose vaguely. He blinked. By a curious effect of light
the headlights of one car and the red taillight of th
other—Mr. Quin seemed for a moment to be dressed i
motley himself. But it was only the light.

"We can't leave you here stranded on the road," cor
tinued Mr. Satterthwaite. "You must come along with u

here's plenty of room for three, isn't there, Melrose?"

"Oh, rather." But the colonel's voice was a little doubt-
ul. "The only thing is," he remarked, "the job we're on.
h, Satterthwaite?"

Mr. Satterthwaite stood stock-still. Ideas leaped and
lashed over him. He positively shook with excitement.

"No," he cried. "No, I should have known better!
There is no chance where you are concerned, Mr. Quin.
t was not an accident that we all met tonight at the
rossroads."

Colonel Melrose stared at his friend in astonishment.
Mr. Satterthwaite took him by the arm.

"You remember what I told you—about our friend
Derek Capel? The motive for his suicide, which no one
could guess? It was Mr. Quin who solved that problem—
and there have been others since. He shows you things
that are there all the time, but which you haven't seen.
He's marvelous."

"My dear Satterthwaite, you are making me blush,"
said Mr. Quin, smiling. "As far as I can remember, these
discoveries were all made by you, not by me."

"They were made because you were there," said Mr.
Satterthwaite with intense conviction.

"Well," said Colonel Melrose, clearing his throat uncomfortably. "We mustn't waste any more time. Let's get
on."

He climbed into the driver's seat. He was not too well
pleased at having the stranger foisted upon him through
Mr. Satterthwaite's enthusiasm, but he had no valid ob-
jection to offer, and he was anxious to get on to Alderway as fast as possible.

Mr. Satterthwaite urged Mr. Quin in next, and himself
took the outside seat. The car was a roomy one and took
three without undue squeezing.

"So you are interested in crime, Mr. Quin?" said the

colonel, doing his best to be genial.

"No, not exactly in crime."

"What, then?"

Mr. Quin smiled. "Let us ask Mr. Satterthwaite. He i
a very shrewd observer."

"I think," said Satterthwaite slowly, "I may be wrong
but I think—that Mr. Quin is interested in—lovers."

He blushed as he said the last word, which is one n
Englishman can pronounce without self-consciousness
Mr. Satterthwaite brought it out apologetically, and wit
an effect of inverted commas.

"By gad!" said the colonel, startled and silenced.

He reflected inwardly that this seemed to be a very
rum friend of Satterthwaite's. He glanced at him side
ways. The fellow looked all right—quite a normal young
chap. Rather dark, but not at all foreign-looking.

"And now," said Satterthwaite importantly, "I mus
tell you all about the case."

He talked for some ten minutes. Sitting there in the
darkness, rushing through the night, he had an intoxi
cating feeling of power. What did it matter if he were
only a looker-on at life? He had words at his command
he was master of them, he could string them to a patterr
—a strange Renaissance pattern composed of the beauty
of Laura Dwighton, with her white arms and red hair—
and the shadowy dark figure of Paul Delangua, whom
women found handsome.

Set that against the background of Alderway—Alderway that had stood since the days of Henry VII and
some said, before that. Alderway that was English to the
core, with its clipped yew and its old beak barn and the
fishpond, where monks had kept their carp for Fridays.

In a few deft strokes he had etched in Sir James, a
Dwighton who was a true descendant of the old De Wit-
tons, who long ago had wrung money out of the land

nd locked it fast in coffers, so that whoever else had
allen on evil days, the masters of Alderway had never
ecome impoverished.

At last Mr. Satterthwaite ceased. He was sure, had been
are all along, of the sympathy of his audience. He waited
ow the word of praise which was his due. It came.

"You are an artist, Mr. Satterthwaite."

"I—I do my best." The little man was suddenly hum-
le.

They had turned in at the lodge gates some minutes
go. Now the car drew up in front of the doorway, and a
olice constable came hurriedly down the steps to meet
hem.

"Good evening, sir. Inspector Curtis is in the library."

"Right."

Melrose ran up the steps followed by the other two. As
he three of them passed across the wide hall, an elderly
utler peered from a doorway apprehensively. Melrose
odded to him.

"Evening, Miles. This is a sad business."

"It is indeed," the other quavered. "I can hardly be-
ieve it, sir; indeed I can't. To think that anyone should
trike down the master."

"Yes, yes," said Melrose, cutting him short. "I'll have
. talk with you presently."

He strode on to the library. There a big, soldierly-
ooking inspector greeted him with respect.

"Nasty business, sir. I have not disturbed things. No
ingerprints on the weapon. Whoever did it knew his
usiness."

Mr. Satterthwaite looked at the bowed figure sitting at
he big writing-table, and looked hurriedly away again.
The man had been struck down from behind, a smash-
ng blow that had crashed in the skull. The sight was not
. pretty one.

The weapon lay on the floor—a bronze figure about two feet high, the base of it stained and wet. Mr. Satterthwaite bent over it curiously.

"A Venus," he said softly. "So he was struck down by Venus."

He found food for poetic meditation in the thought.

"The windows," said the inspector, "were all closed and bolted on the inside."

He paused significantly.

"Making an inside job of it," said the chief constable reluctantly. "Well—well, we'll see."

The murdered man was dressed in golf clothes, and a bag of golf clubs had been flung untidily across a big leather couch.

"Just come in from the links," explained the inspector, following the chief constable's glance. "At five-fifteen that was. Had tea brought here by the butler. Later he rang for his valet to bring him down a pair of soft slippers. As far as we can tell, the valet was the last person to see him alive."

Melrose nodded, and turned his attention once more to the writing-table.

A good many of the ornaments had been overturned and broken. Prominent among these was a big dark enamel clock, which lay on its side in the very center of the table.

The inspector cleared his throat.

"That's what you might call a piece of luck, sir," he said. "As you see, it's stopped. *At half past six.* That gives us the time of the crime. Very convenient."

The colonel was staring at the clock.

"As you say," he remarked. "Very convenient." He paused a minute, and then added, "Too damned convenient! I don't like it, Inspector."

He looked around at the other two. His eye sought

Mr. Quin's with a look of appeal in it.

"Damn it all," he said. "It's too neat. You know what I mean. Things don't happen like that."

"You mean," murmured Mr. Quin, "that clocks don't fall like that?"

Melrose stared at him for a moment, then back at the clock, which had that pathetic and innocent look familiar to objects which have been suddenly bereft of their dignity. Very carefully Colonel Melrose replaced it on its legs again. He struck the table a violent blow. The clock rocked, but it did not fall. Melrose repeated the action, and very slowly, with a kind of unwillingness, the clock fell over on its back.

"What time was the crime discovered?" demanded Melrose sharply.

"Just about seven o'clock, sir."

"Who discovered it?"

"The butler."

"Fetch him in," said the chief constable. "I'll see him now. Where is Lady Dwighton, by the way?"

"Lying down, sir. Her maid says that she's prostrated and can't see anyone."

Melrose nodded, and Inspector Curtis went in search of the butler. Mr. Quin was looking thoughtfully into the fireplace. Mr. Satterthwaite followed his example. He blinked at the smoldering logs for a minute or two, and then something bright lying in the grate caught his eye. He stooped and picked up a little sliver of curved glass.

"You wanted me, sir?"

It was the butler's voice, still quavering and uncertain. Mr. Satterthwaite slipped the fragment of glass into his waistcoat pocket and turned round.

The old man was standing in the doorway.

"Sit down," said the chief constable kindly. "You're shaking all over. It's been a shock to you, I expect."

"It has indeed, sir."

"Well, I shan't keep you long. Your master came in just after five, I believe?"

"Yes, sir. He ordered tea to be brought to him here. Afterward, when I came to take it away, he asked for Jennings to be sent to him—that's his valet, sir."

"What time was that?"

"About ten minutes past six, sir."

"Yes—well?"

"I sent word to Jennings, sir. And it wasn't till I came in here to shut the windows and draw the curtains at seven o'clock that I saw—"

Melrose cut him short. "Yes, yes, you needn't go into all that. You didn't touch the body, or disturb anything, did you?"

"Oh! No indeed, sir! I went as fast as I could go to the telephone to ring up the police."

"And then?"

"I told Janet—her ladyship's maid, sir—to break the news to her ladyship."

"You haven't seen your mistress at all this evening?"

Colonel Melrose put the question casually enough, but Mr. Satterthwaite's keen ears caught anxiety behind the words.

"Not to speak to, sir. Her ladyship has remained in her own apartments since the tragedy."

"Did you see her before?"

The question came sharply, and everyone in the room noted the hesitation before the butler replied.

"I—I just caught a glimpse of her, sir, descending the staircase."

"Did she come in here?"

Mr. Satterthwaite held his breath.

"I—I think so, sir."

"What time was that?"

You might have heard a pin drop. Did the old man know, Mr. Satterthwaite wondered, what hung on his answer?

"It was just upon half past six, sir."

Colonel Melrose drew a deep breath. "That will do, thank you. Just send Jennings, the valet, to me, will you?"

Jennings answered the summons with promptitude. A narrow-faced man with a catlike tread. Something sly and secretive about him.

A man, thought Mr. Satterthwaite, who would easily murder his master if he could be sure of not being found out.

He listened eagerly to the man's answers to Colonel Melrose's questions. But his story seemed straightforward enough. He had brought his master down some soft hide slippers and removed the brogues.

"What did you do after that, Jennings?"

"I went back to the stewards' room, sir."

"At what time did you leave your master?"

"It must have been just after a quarter past six, sir."

"Where were you at half past six, Jennings?"

"In the stewards' room, sir."

Colonel Melrose dismissed the man with a nod. He looked across at Curtis inquiringly.

"Quite correct, sir, I checked that up. He was in the stewards' room from about six-twenty until seven o'clock."

"Then that lets him out," said the chief constable a trifle regretfully. "Besides, there's no motive."

They looked at each other.

There was a tap at the door.

"Come in," said the colonel.

A scared-looking lady's maid appeared.

"If you please, her ladyship has heard that Colonel

Melrose is here and she would like to see him."

"Certainly," said Melrose. "I'll come at once. Will you show me the way?"

But a hand pushed the girl aside. A very different figure now stood in the doorway. Laura Dwighton looked like a visitor from another world.

She was dressed in a clinging medieval tea gown of dull-blue brocade. Her auburn hair parted in the middle and brought down over her ears. Conscious of the fact she had a style of her own, Lady Dwighton had never had her hair cut. It was drawn back into a simple knot in the nape of her neck. Her arms were bare.

One of them was outstretched to steady herself against the frame of the doorway, the other hung down by her side, clasping a book. *She looks,* Mr. Satterthwaite thought, *like a Madonna from an early Italian canvas.*

She stood there, swaying slightly from side to side. Colonel Melrose sprang toward her.

"I've come to tell you—to tell you—"

Her voice was low and rich. Mr. Satterthwaite was so entranced with the dramatic value of the scene that he had forgotten its reality.

"Please, Lady Dwighton—" Melrose had an arm round her, supporting her. He took her across the hall into a small anteroom, its walls hung with faded silk. Quin and Satterthwaite followed. She sank down on the low settee, her head resting back on a rust-colored cushion, her eyelids closed. The three men watched her. Suddenly she opened her eyes and sat up. She spoke very quietly.

"*I killed him,*" she said. "That's what I came to tell you. *I killed him!*"

There was a moment's agonized silence. Mr. Satterthwaite's heart missed a beat.

"Lady Dwighton," said Melrose. "You've had a great shock—you're unstrung. I don't think you quite know what you're saying."

Would she draw back now—while there was yet time?

"I know perfectly what I'm saying. It was I who shot him."

Two of the men in the room gasped, the other made no sound. Laura Dwighton leaned still farther forward.

"Don't you understand? I came down and shot him. I admit it."

The book she had been holding in her hand clattered to the floor. There was a paper cutter in it, a thing shaped like a dagger with a jeweled hilt. Mr. Satterthwaite picked it up mechanically and placed it on the table. As he did so he thought, *That's a dangerous toy. You could kill a man with that.*

"Well—" Laura Dwighton's voice was impatient— "what are you going to do about it? Arrest me? Take me away?"

Colonel Melrose found his voice with difficulty.

"What you have told me is very serious, Lady Dwighton. I must ask you to go to your room till I have—er—made arrangements."

She nodded and rose to her feet. She was quite composed now, grave and cold.

As she turned toward the door, Mr. Quin spoke. "What did you do with the revolver, Lady Dwighton?"

A flicker of uncertainty passed across her face. "I—I dropped it there on the floor. No, I think I threw it out of the window—oh! I can't remember now. What does it matter? I hardly knew what I was doing. It doesn't matter, does it?"

"No," said Mr. Quin. "I hardly think it matters."

She looked at him in perplexity with a shade of something that might have been alarm. Then she flung back her head and went imperiously out of the room. Mr. Satterthwaite hastened after her. She might, he felt, collapse at any minute. But she was already halfway up the staircase, displaying no sign of her earlier weakness. The scared-looking maid was standing at the foot of the stairway, and Mr. Satterthwaite spoke to her authoritatively.

"Look after your mistress," he said.

"Yes, sir." The girl prepared to ascend after the blue-robed figure. "Oh, please, sir, they don't suspect him, do they?"

"Suspect whom?"

"Jennings, sir. Oh! Indeed, sir, he wouldn't hurt a fly."

"Jennings? No, of course not. Go and look after your mistress."

"Yes, sir."

The girl ran quickly up the staircase. Mr. Satterthwaite returned to the room he had just vacated.

Colonel Melrose was saying heavily, "Well, I'm jiggered. There's more in this than meets the eye. It—it's like those dashed silly things heroines do in many novels."

"It's unreal," agreed Mr. Satterthwaite. "It's like something on the stage."

Mr. Quin nodded. "Yes, you admire the drama, do you not? You are a man who appreciates good acting when you see it."

Mr. Satterthwaite looked hard at him.

In the silence that followed a far-off sound came to their ears.

"Sounds like a shot," said Colonel Melrose. "One of the keepers, I daresay. That's probably what she heard. Perhaps she went down to see. She wouldn't go close or examine the body. She'd leap at once to the conclusion—"

"Mr. Delangua, sir." It was the old butler who spoke, standing apologetically in the doorway.

"Eh?" said Melrose. "What's that?"

"Mr. Delangua is here, sir, and would like to speak to

you if he may."

Colonel Melrose leaned back in his chair. "Show him in," he said grimly.

A moment later Paul Delangua stood in the doorway. As Colonel Melrose had hinted, there was something un-English about him—the easy grace of his movements, the dark, handsome face, the eyes set a little too near together. There hung about him the air of the Renaissance. He and Laura Dwighton suggested the same atmosphere.

"Good evening, gentlemen," said Delangua. He made a little theatrical bow.

"I don't know what your business may be, Mr. Delangua," said Colonel Melrose sharply, "but if it is nothing to do with the matter at hand—"

Delangua interrupted him with a laugh. "On the contrary," he said, "it has everything to do with it."

"What do you mean?"

"I mean," said Delangua quietly, "that I have come to give myself up for the murder of Sir James Dwighton."

"You know what you are saying?" said Melrose gravely.

"Perfectly."

The young man's eyes were riveted to the table.

"I don't understand—"

"Why I give myself up? Call it remorse—call it anything you please. I stabbed him, right enough—you may be quite sure of that." He nodded toward the table. "You've got the weapon there, I see. A very handy little tool. Lady Dwighton unfortunately left it lying around in a book, and I happened to snatch it up."

"One minute," said Colonel Melrose. "Am I to understand that you admit stabbing Sir James with this?" He held the dagger aloft.

"Quite right. I stole in through the window, you know. He had his back to me. It was quite easy. I left the same way."

"Through the window?"

"Through the window, of course."

"And what time was this?"

Delangua hesitated. "Let me see—I was talking to the keeper fellow—that was at a quarter past six. I heard the church tower chime. It must have been—well, say somewhere about half past."

A grim smile came to the colonel's lips.

"Quite right, young man," he said. "Half past six was the time. Perhaps you've heard that already? But this is altogether a most peculiar murder!"

"Why?"

"So many people confess to it," said Colonel Melrose.

They heard the sharp intake of the other's breath.

"Who else has confessed to it?" he asked in a voice that he vainly strove to render steady.

"Lady Dwighton."

Delangua threw back his head and laughed in rather a forced manner. "Lady Dwighton is apt to be hysterical," he said lightly. "I shouldn't pay any attention to what she says if I were you."

"I don't think I shall," said Melrose. "But there's another odd thing about this murder."

"What's that?"

"Well," said Melrose, "Lady Dwighton has confessed to having shot Sir James, and you have confessed to having stabbed him. But luckily for both of you, he wasn't shot or stabbed, you see. His skull was smashed in."

"My God!" cried Delangua. "But a woman couldn't possibly do that—"

He stopped, biting his lip. Melrose nodded with the ghost of a smile.

"Often read of it," he volunteered. "Never seen it happen."

"What?"

"Couple of young idiots each accusing themselves because they thought the other had done it," said Melrose. "Now we've got to begin at the beginning."

"The valet," cried Mr. Satterthwaite. "That girl just now—I wasn't paying any attention at the time." He paused, striving for coherence. "She was afraid of our suspecting him. There must be some motive that he had and which we don't know, but she does."

Colonel Melrose frowned, then he rang the bell. When it was answered, he said, "Please ask Lady Dwighton if she will be good enough to come down again."

They waited in silence until she came. At sight of Delangua she started and stretched out a hand to save herself from falling. Colonel Melrose came quickly to the rescue.

"It's quite all right, Lady Dwighton. Please don't be alarmed."

"I don't understand. What is Mr. Delangua doing here?"

Delangua came over to her. "Laura—Laura—why did you do it?"

"Do it?"

"I know. It was for me—because you thought that I— After all, it was natural, I suppose. But, oh! You angel!"

Colonel Melrose cleared his throat. He was a man who disliked emotion and had a horror of anything approaching a "scene."

"If you'll allow me to say so, Lady Dwighton, both you and Mr. Delangua have had a lucky escape. He had just arrived in his turn to 'confess' to the murder—oh, it's quite all right, he didn't do it! But what we want to know is the truth. No more shillyshallying. The butler says you went into the library at half past six—is that so?"

Laura looked at Delangua. He nodded.

"The truth, Laura," he said. "That is what we want now."

She breathed a deep sigh. "I will tell you."

She sank down on a chair that Mr. Satterthwaite had hurriedly pushed forward.

"I did come down. I opened the library door and I saw—"

She stopped and swallowed. Mr. Satterthwaite leaned forward and patted her hand encouragingly.

"Yes," he said. "Yes. You saw?"

"My husband was lying across the writing-table. I saw his head—the blood—oh!"

She put her hands to her face. The chief constable leaned forward.

"Excuse me, Lady Dwighton. You thought Mr. Delangua had shot him?"

She nodded. "Forgive me, Paul," she pleaded. "But you said—you said—"

"That I'd shoot him like a dog," said Delangua grimly. "I remember. That was the day I discovered he'd been ill-treating you."

The chief constable kept sternly to the matter in hand.

"Then I am to understand, Lady Dwighton, that you went upstairs again and—er—said nothing. We needn't go into your reason. You didn't touch the body or go near the writing-table?"

She shuddered.

"No, no. I ran straight out of the room."

"I see, I see. And what time was this exactly? Do you know?"

"It was just half past six when I got back to my bedroom."

"Then at—say five-and-twenty past six, Sir James was already dead." The chief constable looked at the others. "That clock—it was faked, eh? We suspected that all along. Nothing easier than to move the hands to whatever time you wished, but they made a mistake to lay it down on its side like that. Well, that seems to narrow it down to the butler or the valet, and I can't believe it's the butler. Tell me, Lady Dwighton, did this man Jennings have any grudge against your husband?"

Laura lifted her face from her hands. "Not exactly a grudge, but—well James told me only this morning that he'd dismissed him. He'd found him pilfering."

"Ah! Now we're getting at it. Jennings would have been dismissed without a character. A serious matter for him."

"You said something about a clock," said Laura Dwighton. "There's just a chance—if you want to fix the time—James would have been sure to have his little golf watch on him. Mightn't that have been smashed, too, when he fell forward?"

"It's an idea," said the colonel slowly. "But I'm afraid —Curtis!"

The inspector nodded in quick comprehension and left the room. He returned a minute later. On the palm of his hand was a silver watch marked like a golf ball, the kind that are sold for golfers to carry loose in a pocket with balls.

"Here it is, sir," he said, "but I doubt if it will be any good. They're tough, these watches."

The colonel took it from him and held it to his ear.

"It seems to have stopped, anyway," he observed.

He pressed with his thumb, and the lid of the watch flew open. Inside the glass was cracked across.

"Ah!" he said exultantly.

The hand pointed to exactly a quarter past six.

"A very good glass of port, Colonel Melrose," said Mr. Quin.

It was half past nine, and the three men had just fin ished a belated dinner at Colonel Melrose's house. Mr Satterthwaite was particularly jubilant.

"I was quite right," he chuckled. "You can't deny it Mr. Quin. You turned up tonight to save two absurd young people who were both bent on putting their heads into a noose."

"Did I?" said Mr. Quin. "Surely not. I did nothing at all."

"As it turned out, it was not necessary," agreed Mr Satterthwaite. "But it might have been. It was touch and go, you know. I shall never forget the moment when Lady Dwighton said, 'I killed him.' I've never seen any thing on the stage half as dramatic."

"I'm inclined to agree with you," said Mr. Quin.

"Wouldn't have believed such a thing could happen outside a novel," declared the colonel, for perhaps the twentieth time that night.

"Does it?" asked Mr. Quin.

The colonel stared at him. "Damn it, it happened to-night."

"Mind you," interposed Mr. Satterthwaite, leaning back and sipping his port. "Lady Dwighton was mag nificent, quite magnificent, but she made one mistake. She shouldn't have leaped to the conclusion that her husband had been shot. In the same way Delangua was a fool to assume that he had been stabbed just because the dagger happened to be lying on the table in front of us. It was a mere coincidence that Lady Dwighton should have brought it down with her."

"Was it?" asked Mr. Quin.

"Now if they'd only confined themselves to saying that they'd killed Sir James, without particularizing how—" went on Mr. Satterthwaite—"what would have been the result?"

"They might have been believed," said Mr. Quin with an odd smile.

"The whole thing was exactly like a novel," said the colonel.

"That's where they got the idea from, I daresay," said Mr. Quin.

"Possibly," agreed Mr. Satterthwaite. "Things one has read do come back to one in the oddest way." He looked across at Mr. Quinn. "Of course," he said, "the clock really looked suspicious from the first. One ought never to forget how easy it is to put the hands of a clock or watch forward or back."

Mr. Quin nodded and repeated the words. "Forward," he said, and paused. "Or back."

There was something encouraging in his voice. His bright, dark eyes were fixed on Mr. Satterthwaite.

"The hands of the clock were put forward," said Mr. Satterthwaite. "We know that."

"Were they?" asked Mr. Quin.

Mr. Satterthwaite stared at him. "Do you mean," he said slowly, "that it was the watch which was put back? But that doesn't make sense. It's impossible."

"Not impossible," murmured Mr. Quin.

"Well—absurd. To whose advantage could that be?"

"Only, I suppose, to someone who had an *alibi* for that time."

"By gad!" cried the colonel. "That's the time young Delangua said he was talking to the keeper."

"He told us that very particularly," said Mr. Satterthwaite.

They looked at each other. They had an uneasy feeling as of solid ground failing beneath their feet. Facts went spinning round, turning new and unexpected faces. And in the center of the kaleidoscope was the dark, smiling face of Mr. Quin.

"But in that case—" began Melrose—"in that case—"

Mr. Satterthwaite, nimble-witted, finished his sentence for him. "It's all the other way round. A plant just the same—but a plant against the valet. Oh, but it can't be! It's impossible. Why each of them accused themselves of the crime."

"Yes," said Mr. Quin. "Up till then you suspected them, didn't you?" His voice went on, placid and dreamy. "Just like something out of a book, you said, colonel. They got the idea there. It's what the innocent hero and heroine do. Of course it made you think them innocent —there was the force of tradition behind them. Mr. Satterthwaite has been saying all along it was like something on the stage. You were both right. It wasn't real. You've been saying so all along without knowing what you were saying. They'd have told a much better story than that if they'd wanted to be believed."

The two men looked at him helplessly.

"It would be clever," said Mr. Satterthwaite slowly. "It would be diabolically clever. And I've thought of something else. The butler said he went in at seven to shut the windows—so he must have expected them to be open."

"That's the way Delangua came in," said Mr. Quin. "He killed Sir James with one blow, and he and she together did what they had to do—"

He looked at Mr. Satterthwaite, encouraging him to reconstruct the scene. He did so, hesitatingly.

"They smashed the clock and put it on its side. Yes. They altered the watch and smashed it. Then he went out of the window, and she fastened it after him. But there's one thing I don't see. Why bother with the watch at all? Why not simply put back the hands of the clock?"

"The clock was always a little obvious," said Mr. Quin.

THREE BLIND MICE   223

"Anyone might have seen through a rather transparent device like that."

"But surely the watch was too farfetched. Why, it was pure chance that we ever thought of the watch."

"Oh, no," said Mr. Quin. "It was the lady's suggestion, remember."

Mr. Satterthwaite stared at him, fascinated.

"And yet, you know," said Mr. Quin dreamily, "the one person who wouldn't be likely to overlook the watch would be the valet. Valets know better than anyone what their masters carry in their pockets. If he altered the clock, the valet would have altered the watch, too. They don't understand human nature, those two. They are not like Mr. Satterthwaite."

Mr. Satterthwaite shook his head.

"I was all wrong," he murmured humbly. "I thought that you had come to save them."

"So I did," said Mr. Quin. "Oh! Not those two—the others. Perhaps you didn't notice the lady's maid? She wasn't wearing blue brocade, or acting a dramatic part. But she's really a very pretty girl, and I think she loves that man Jennings very much. I think that between you you'll be able to save her man from getting hanged."

"We've no proof of any kind," said Colonel Melrose heavily.

Mr. Quin smiled. "Mr. Satterthwaite has."

"I?" Mr. Satterthwaite was astonished.

Mr. Quin went on. "You've got a proof that that watch wasn't smashed in Sir James's pocket. You can't smash a watch like that without opening the case. Just try it and see. Someone took the watch out and opened it, set back the hands, smashed the glass, and then shut it and put it back. They never noticed that a fragment of glass was missing."

"Oh!" cried Mr. Satterthwaite. His hand flew to his

waistcoat pocket. He drew out a fragment of curved glass.

It was his moment.

"With this," said Mr. Satterthwaite importantly, "I shall save a man from death."